Mills & B...

A chance to read and collect some of the best-loved novels from Mills & Boon—the world's largest publisher of romantic fiction.

Every month, four titles by favourite Mills & Boon authors will be re-published in the *Classics* series.

A list of other titles in the *Classics* series can be found at the end of this book.

Elizabeth Hunter

THE BEADS OF NEMESIS

MILLS & BOON LIMITED
LONDON · TORONTO

First published 1974
Australian copyright 1980
Philippine copyright 1980
This edition 1980

© Elizabeth Hunter 1974

ISBN 0 263 73474 9

Set in 10 pt. Monotype Plantin

Made and printed in Great Britain by Richard Clay (The Chaucer Press) Ltd, Bungay, Suffolk

For Mrs. Meryl Farrington,
and for her family who kindly loaned
me her company for eight days in Greece.

Nemesis was the compensating goddess, measuring out happiness and misery. She took especial care of the presumptuous, punishing *hubris*, the crime of considering oneself master of one's own destiny. She was known also by the surnames of Adrastia (inescapable) and of Rhamnousia, from her sanctuary at Rhamnous. Associated with the worship of Nemesis was Themis, the goddess who personified law, equity and custom.

Blue Guide on Greece, page 216
Published by Ernest Benn Ltd.

CHAPTER ONE

THE little village of Marathon wilted under the hot sun. Even the breeze, such as it was, did no more than disturb the dust at the corners of the narrow streets, blowing its hot breath on the few plants that struggled in the heat, scorching the dry leaves into a uniform brown. Morag Grant stepped off the pavement and narrowly missed being run over by an army truck that came hurtling round the corner. It was the only sign of life she had seen.

Once more she consulted the guide-book in her knapsack, easing her shoulders from the strain of carrying the heavy bag. It would take her three hours to walk to Rhamous, she thought. Three hours in this blazing heat and on an empty stomach. She made a face at the printed word which had not changed at all from when she had last looked at it. Would it be worth going all that way? She had thought so that morning in Athens, when she had thought that anything would be better than staying in the sultry atmosphere of the city. Now, she was not so sure. These things were fun when one had company to complain to, and to laugh with at the shared complaints; on her own, she found she was lonely and dispirited even by the prospect of enjoying herself.

Morag picked up her knapsack again with her left hand and wandered into the relative coolness of one of the shops.

"*Kaliméra,*" she murmured to the black-clad woman who sat behind the counter in the dim light.

"*Kaliméra sas,*" the woman answered.

Morag pointed to a bottle of fizzy lemonade. "Please," she said, and then again: "*Parakaló.*"

The woman picked out one of the bottles and opened it it with a practised movement of her wrist, pushing the lem-

7

onade across the counter together with a wrapped straw for Morag to drink from. *"Deutsch?"* she asked.

Morag shook her head. "English," she answered. She wondered if she looked German, or if it was because by far the greatest number of tourists in Greece were from Germany, but the enquiry about her nationality seemed to have followed her around ever since she had arrived.

The woman favoured her with a slow smile. *"Kalá!"* She blew out her cheeks and shook the front of her black blouse, signifying that it was hot. Morag nodded eagerly, putting off the moment when she would have to go back outside into the blinding heat for as long as possible.

But in the end she had no further excuse for delay and she stepped out into the shimmering whiteness of the street, blinking at the sudden excess of light. It was not very far down the Athens road where she had to turn off on to the smaller road to Rhamous, but by the time she had reached it she was already hot and sticky and the straps of her knapsack had rubbed her shoulders raw. With determination, she gritted her teeth and set herself the next measure of the walk before she would allow herself to rest again.

So set she was on completing the distance she had decided upon that she barely noticed the car as it drew up beside her.

"Want a lift?" a masculine voice asked her.

She started, pausing to wipe the sweat out of her eyes. *Of course* she wanted a lift! But she wasn't sure if it would be wise to accept, all the same, and stood in an agony of indecision by the side of the road, trying to make up her mind. The two children in the back were a decided plus, and the right-hand drive telling its own story that this was a British car was another one. But the man didn't look English. Far from it. His black, curly hair gave him an exotic look that was further accentuated by the width of his shoulders and the cut of his shirt that was only done up by the last button revealing an expanse of tanned chest set off by a golden crucifix of the Greek type, with Christ regnant and vested

8

on the front. He was a minus factor, she decided, though a mightily attractive one.

"Get in!" he said.

"But – " she began, then hesitated. "Are you going to Rhamous?"

"Get in!" he said again with increasing impatience.

She looked down at her knapsack, a little put out when the man merely grinned and, getting slowly out of the car, lifted it with an ease that made her own struggles with the thing seem pointless. "Do you want it with you, or shall I put it up on the roof-rack?" he asked her.

She found herself saying something about putting it wherever it would be more convenient to him and hurried into the front passenger seat. "Hullo," she said to the children. They were very alike to look at, with practically the same hair-style, though one was clearly a boy and the other a girl.

"Hullo," they responded. The girl broke into a wide smile. "Were you afraid of Daddy?" she demanded, her eyes twinkling. "I told him he ought to cut his hair before we get to Grandma's house."

"Several times," the girl's father put in wryly, getting back into the car. "All right, I'm convinced, I look like Barbarossa himself –"

"Not Barbarossa!" Morag said. "He must have had a red beard!"

"And mine, if I had one, is black," the man agreed. He smiled at Morag in a strangely intimate way, as if he knew her well, and she was surprised to discover a little fountain of excitement within her that responded to his look in a way she had not known for a long, long time. "Will you cut it for me in exchange for transporting you to Rhamous?" he suggested.

Morag swallowed. "If you like," she said.

"I think I might like it very much," he answered imperturbably. "My name is Pericles Holmes. Most people call

9

me Perry. The two in the back are Kimon and Peggy."

"How d'you do?" said Morag, still a little uncertain. Surely it hadn't been as long as all that since she had last sat beside an attractive man and talked nonsense with him? Surely she wasn't going to be *shy*? She took a determined hold on herself. "I'm Morag Grant."

She waited for him to recognise the name, but he showed no sign of having done so and she took a quick breath of relief.

"Pretty name," was all he said.

"It isn't English, but then I'm really a Scot," she explained. "Only I've always lived in England."

"We're a bit Scottish too," Kimon informed her. "But we're more Greek. Grandma is Greek and Mummy was half Greek too."

"Was?" Morag said before she could stop herself.

"She's dead," Peggy said in carefully matter-of-fact tones. "I don't suppose one keeps one's nationality when one is dead, do you think? That's why Kimon said she *was* half-Greek. She was half British too."

Morag thought she heard a faintly wistful note in the last few words and smiled at the little girl, turning her head to see her the better. "My mother is dead too," she said. "I can't remember her at all. My father married again and my stepmother had a little girl too. We were brought up together."

"Kimon and I are twins," Peggy volunteered.

"That must be why you look alike," said Morag.

Peggy's eyes flashed. "We're not *identical* twins. If we were, we'd both be girls —"

"Or boys!" Kimon interrupted. "It would be better if we were both boys. *Then* we wouldn't have to live with Grandma!"

"That's enough, Kimon," their father interposed. "Morag was telling us about her family. Go on, Morag."

"There isn't anything more to say," she answered. "My

10

stepsister and I are the same age, so I suppose we might as well have been twins too."

"Only you didn't like her much, did you?" Pericles Holmes observed. "Why not? Did she tell tales to her mother? Or was it something worse than that?"

The children giggled. Evidently that was considered the most heinous crime that either of them could commit.

"I didn't *dis*like her," Morag compromised. "I suppose we didn't have much in common."

Pericles lifted his eyebrows, giving his face a knowing look that disturbed her strangely. "No?"

She cast him a swift look from beneath her lashes. "You can't dislike someone you live with for years. You have to come to some arrangement so that you don't," she confided. "It's very wearing disliking people and it doesn't do any good."

Pericles' smile mocked her. "That sounds a very profound thought. You have us all disliking her now on your behalf," he added with a laugh. "Tell us more about her. I like to know my enemy! Is she a blonde like you?"

"No." Morag looked embarrassed. "Her looks are more definite than mine, if you know what I mean. She's much better looking than I am."

Pericles laughed. "I prefer a pretty blonde myself, being dark —"

Black and beautiful she would have called him, Morag thought.

She struggled hastily back into speech before he could guess at her inner turmoil and wonder, as she was already doing, at the reason for it. "I'm not really blonde either! I'm nothing in particular!"

His eyes swept over her. "Perhaps in an English winter. But the sun has bleached your hair nicely since you've been out here. Perhaps you haven't noticed?"

She ran a hand over her hair as if it offended her. "I've been camping. Does it look awful?"

11

His eyes twinkled. "I'd call that a leading question," he teased her. "I suppose you have a tent in that knapsack of yours?" He frowned as she nodded in agreement. "Where are your companions?"

"I haven't any," she said.

"Greece is no place for a young woman on her own —"

"Perhaps not. But it really isn't any of your business, is it?" she retorted.

"I'm making it my business," he drawled, ignoring her angry face. "What happened to your friends?"

She bit her lip. "I was – held up. The others had all gone by the time I was ready, so I came on my own. I *like* my own company!"

"Like hell you do!"

Morag glared at him, holding on to her temper with a conscious effort. Was it so obvious that she had hated being on her own? She pursed up her lips and studied her fingers carefully, noticing that they were brown from the sun and that she had torn one of her nails.

"There's Rhamous just round the corner. I'd say you've come to the right place, Morag Grant. Play your cards right and Nemesis will make it up to you for all you've had to suffer in the past."

Morag was startled out of her anger. "Nemesis? I thought she went in for retribution?"

She considered rebuking him for his use of her first name, but something told her that she would probably regret it if she did. "I know what it is to be unhappy," she said, "most of us do."

"Unfortunately," he agreed. "But most of us are older than you are when we make that discovery. You don't look much older than Kimon and Peggy!"

But she was older – aeons older than they! She smiled briefly, opting out of the conversation. "I think I'll read it up before I go on to the site," she said instead. "I like to know what I'm looking at."

"You don't have to do that with Daddy," Kimon informed her. "He tells us all about the places we visit. He knows them all without having to look at any book!"

Morag didn't look up. "How come?" she asked.

"It's my job," Pericles said simply. "I start work this autumn with the local archaeological society. Before that I had a job with the British Museum."

"But now we have to live *here*," Peggy sighed. "We have to live with Grandma, and it's perfectly horrid!"

"Oh dear," said Morag.

"It's worse even than that," Kimon finished for his sister. "We wouldn't have to if Peggy wasn't a girl!"

"Why should that make any difference?" Morag asked, genuinely bewildered.

"Daddy says he can't bring her up on his own," he said moodily. "She has to have a woman around. Only she wouldn't ask Grandma anything anyway, because no one would." He broke off abruptly with a meaning look at Peggy. "Daddy's bought the tickets, so hush up. He doesn't like it when we go on about not wanting to live with Grandma. He can't think of anything else to do with us."

Morag's sympathy was caught. She knew only too well what it was like to have to live with relations who put up with one rather than love one, and who plainly wished you somewhere else. She was touched too by Pericles Holmes' concern for his daughter. It showed, she thought, an unusual sensitivity to her needs to want to have a woman take a hand in her upbringing. Her own father had remarried for quite different reasons and had ended by preferring his stepdaughter to his own prickly child – but no doubt he was not wholly to blame for that!

He touched her on her arm and she pulled away from him as if his touch had burned her. "I'm sorry," she said. "I was thinking."

"You think too much," he observed. "In Greece you have to feel, not think all the time. Particularly not sad

13

thoughts. Here's your ticket. Come with us and I'll explain what you have to do to gain the favour of Nemesis."

He brought his hand from behind his back and grasped her arm firmly with the other one. With a seriousness that intrigued her, he put a shell necklace over her head and arranged it against the opening of her shirt. "The boy who sells the tickets was making them for sale," he told her. "I have one for Peggy too. The beads of Nemesis. The plastic ones are a bit modern to appeal, I imagine, but the shells should catch her eye. What are you going to ask of her, Morag Grant?"

"I don't know," she admitted. She felt uncomfortable about accepting the necklace, but he had made it very difficult for her to refuse it. "I hadn't really realised that it was her temple here. I just came."

"I expect she'll forgive you." There was no hint of a smile, so she couldn't be sure if he meant what he said or not.

"Are you sure she doesn't follow you around like – like fate catching up with you?" She wasn't convinced she wanted to gain Nemesis' attention. She didn't trust her, no matter what Pericles said about her.

"The head of her statue that used to be in her temple here is in the British Museum," he smiled. "I got rather fond of her." He flicked the shells on her throat with one finger. "I believe you're scared, Morag. That'll never do! The Holmes family are here to protect you, you know. You don't have to be afraid any more."

She walked behind him up the short path, revelling in the cool wind that blew against her skin. "What makes you think I'm afraid?" she asked.

"It shows in your eyes. What happened, Morag?"

"I was fined for dangerous driving," she heard herself say. She hadn't meant to tell him. She hadn't meant to tell *anyone*! She had been so sure that she could put it behind her and never refer to it again. Why couldn't she? Why did she have to go blabbing about her troubles to any stranger she came across? She could have bitten out her tongue. She had wanted Pericles Holmes to think well of her. It had been important to her, though why she wasn't prepared to think about. "I pleaded guilty."

Pericles sent the children running ahead of them with a single gesture of one hand. He might have an English surname, she thought, but his Greek name suited him far better!

"You've told me too much, or not enough," he said quietly. "If you were guilty, why are you kicking so hard against what happened to you?"

She was dismayed to feel the tears pouring down her cheeks and hated herself for showing such weakness. "My fiancé died in the crash," she said simply.

Pericles looked surprised. "I'm sorry. What kind of man was he?"

"Does it matter?"

"I think it does," he said bluntly.

"Why? Why should it matter to you?" she demanded.

"You won't like it if I tell you," he said with a slight smile. "I suppose he was much older than you –"

"Wrong! He was two years older, if you must know. He was a *splendid* person!"

Pericles looked doubtful. "I don't believe you would have married him in the end. He may have been the most wonderful individual on earth, but he didn't know how to awaken you!" He swung round to face her, looking straight into her eyes, his own alight with a brilliance that made her shake inwardly. "Did he?"

"I loved him –"

"I don't believe you!"

"You don't have to!" she retorted. Her eyes fell before his. "We were both in love with him, only it was me he asked to marry him!"

"What a triumph for you!" His sarcasm made her flush

15

with anger. It hadn't been like that! "Well?" he shouted at her.

"He went out with us both," she said.

"I'll bet!"

She sighed. Nothing could stop the flood of words that she knew was about to break out of her. She had kept silent for so long, but she couldn't resist the look in this man's eyes. If he had been one of the men who had questioned her and questioned her as to what had happened on that awful night, she would have been quite unable to keep silent.

"I did it for David. I knew he was regretting that he had asked me to marry him –"

"Just as you were regretting having accepted him?" Pericles put in dryly.

"I don't know! I never thought of it like that. All I knew was that he was unhappy and that he didn't love me. If we went on as we were, he wouldn't even like me, and I didn't want that. I knew he wanted Delia. That was the hard part, because Delia will never love anyone very much. But he wanted her, so I made up my mind that he should have her."

Pericles shook his head at her. "Now that Nemesis could not approve. That, my dear, is the sin of *hubris*, of thinking that you can manage your own life and other people's without any help from anyone else." He paused to allow her to take in the glorious view from the fallen stones of the temple, pointing out a handy piece of masonry in the shade of a pine-tree where they could sit and stare to their hearts' content at the deep blue of the sea, enclosed by harsh, barren mountains slashed by purple shadows and, in the foreground, the ruined walls of the ancient town that had once had its own fort to defend it, and the dark green of the pine-trees the scent of which vied with the thyme at their feet to give flavour to the refreshing breeze.

"Were you driving the car?" he asked when the silence

had begun to bother her.

Morag gave him a quick glance. "How did you know?"

He shrugged. "I could say you don't look capable of driving dangerously, but I think you are," he said slowly. "But then your sense of justice wouldn't be outraged. I think you might be silly enough to shield someone else, and feminine enough to resent it when you are believed."

"I'm not a complete fool!" she protested.

"Are you not?"

She was silent for a long moment. "I suppose I am," she admitted. "But if David loved her, the least I could do was to protect her – or so I thought. Delia was going to say David had been driving anyway and he had been drinking – they both had! Imagine how his parents would have felt if they'd blamed their dead son for the crash. I think I was right to spare them that."

"No matter what the cost to yourself?"

She blinked. "I thought the price would be worth it."

He pulled down the corner of his mouth. "My dear girl, you haven't begun to pay it. You'd better hurry up and pay your curtsey to Nemesis before you succeed in ruining your whole life! Come on and I'll introduce you."

He made no attempt to help her as she clambered on to the floor of the larger of the two temples, the one nearer to the sea, which was whiter and looked as if it had been built at a later date than the smaller ruin that clung to its side. She had expected some word of sympathy from him, a pat on the back because she had chosen such a hard path and had suffered because of it. But he merely thought her a fool, and that hurt more than it should.

"Mr. Holmes, I don't know what it has to do with you, but I'd do the same again. I heard them crash. It was just below our garden – and it was so easy to change places with Delia. Nothing mattered very much to me just then, with David dead. There didn't seem to be any future for me anyway."

17

"And what about your parents, Miss Grant? Didn't it matter that they would suffer on your behalf?"

She shook her head. "It would have been worse if they'd known it was Delia. It was all that they expected of me."

"That sounds as though you're feeling sorry for yourself," he observed, bending down to take a closer look at one of the fallen Doric columns.

"I suppose I am," she admitted. "I thought coming to Greece would solve all my problems. That I'd feel differently about things – about being me! But I don't. My father doesn't want me home and I don't know where else to go."

"Then that's one problem solved," Pericles told her. "You can tag along with us for a while –"

"But you don't know anything about me!" she said.

"What do you want me to know?"

She tried to marshal her thoughts into some sort of order. "I'm good with children," she said finally. "But I can't give you any references. And how will you explain me to your mother? And supposing the children don't want to have me tagging along? You'd do far better to let me go on by myself."

"Camping on your own in Greece? My dear girl, try and have a little sense! I meant to take you back to Athens with us anyway. It'll suit me very well to have you along –"

"You mean the children might settle better if someone else was there?"

He looked up, smiling. "Something like that."

She sat down on a base of a column, made uncertain by the swift turn of events. Her heart hammered within her, the fountain of excitement within her exploding into a new delight. "I'll try to act as a buffer between them and their grandmother," she found herself saying. "I'll do everything I can –"

"I'm sure you will!" he cut her off. He stood up straight, standing over her in a way that made her look hastily away from him. "You don't have to be grateful," he drawled, sounding amused. "As far as I'm concerned you're the answer to a prayer and I mean to take advantage of you and the situation your crazy stupidity has landed you in to make use of you entirely for my own ends. I can't offer you any references either, you know."

"Oh, but you have the children!" she protested.

"And that's enough for you to trust me to look after you as well?"

She bit her lip aware that he was teasing her. Then she nodded her head. "Yes," she said.

"God help you!" he grinned. "Someone ought to!" He held out his hand to her. "All right, Morag Grant, welcome to the Holmes family."

She put her hand in his and was immediately aware of the strength of his fingers and the smooth warmth of his skin. "Thank you," she said.

He bent his head and kissed her lightly on the lips. "That's to seal the bargain," he told her.

Her colour came and went and she swallowed hard, trying to control her trembling mouth. But he had already turned away, striding across the marble floor of the temple to take a closer look at the smaller one that stood by its side. There was no doubt, she thought, that she was mad to go with him, but how lovely it was to be totally mad for once and to follow her own inclinations, without a thought for anyone else! David she had loved, but David hadn't scared her, nor had he made her feel as though she had run a long race and had finally come home. This one could hurt her as she had not been hurt before. The knowledge came to her as if someone outside herself had spoken the words. A warning from Nemesis? She smiled at the fancy. Hadn't David hurt her by preferring someone else, by preferring Delia whom she had never been able to bring herself to like? Why then should she be afraid of Pericles Holmes?

The boy who had let them into the site whistled to his goats to follow him across the rough ground to where his family kept their hives, weighted down with rocks on the top against the wind. The bells round the goats' necks set off a carillon of sound, deep and melodious, and the cicadas set up their shrill love-song from the other side of a clump of bushes. It was very peaceful there, like an unexpected benison after the turbulent events of the last few months. It was a new beginning and she was glad. She was even more glad that she had taken it into her head to visit Rhamous.

Kimon and Pericles went down to the headland to look at the fort. Peggy refused point blank to go with them.

"I want to stay with Morag," she muttered defiantly to her father. "I *like* Morag!"

"I like Morag too," Kimon chimed in. "But I'd like to see the fort. The view from down there must be terrific!"

"Do you want to go?" Peggy demanded, tugging at Morag's jeans. "Wouldn't you rather sit here quietly with me?"

Morag abandoned the strong desire that she felt to run as fast as she could to the headland – to get there before Pericles and to have him show her the ruins of the ancient town that had once made such an impact on the local life round about. "I'd love to stay with you!" she claimed warmly, smiling at Peggy. "Where shall we sit?"

Pericles cast a quizzical look. "Peggy misses Susan every now and then," he said.

Peggy frowned at him. "I don't. Not really. But I don't like looking at forts. People were killed there – and I don't like that."

"Animals were killed outside the temples as sacrifices," Kimon put in. "I like that even less!"

"But not nowadays," his sister retorted. "Nowadays we get things. If Morag's and my necklaces were a gift from Nemesis –"

"Daddy paid for them!" Kimon pointed out.

"He did not!" Peggy tore the shells loose and scattered them over the ground. "If he did, it's a cheat, and I don't want them!"

Pericles took a long, level look at his daughter and, without a word, strode away from her towards the fort with a rather hesitant Kimon at his heels.

"Now I've made him cross again," Peggy sighed. "He thinks it's because I can't get used to Mummy being dead, but it isn't that. Did you know your mother?" she asked, picking up one of the shells and playing with it between her fingers. "Did you, Morag?"

Morag shook her head. "Sometimes I think I can remember her, but sometimes I know I can't. There was a photograph of her once, but my stepmother got rid of it."

She saw that Peggy's eyes were wet. "Did your father love your stepmother more than your mother?"

"I don't know," Morag answered. "Perhaps. My stepsister is very like her mother and he loves her very much."

The child sighed. "I can't always remember Mummy," she confessed. "I tried not to remember her because Grandma chose her to marry Daddy. Only Kimon says it's wicked. Are you wicked too, Morag?"

"Often and often," Morag agreed, smiling. "Would you like my necklace in place of yours? You could think of it as a present from your mother, if you don't like to have it as a gift from Nemesis."

Peggy accepted the shell necklace and put it round her neck. "Don't tell Daddy," she said solemnly. "Nobody ever understood before. I *hate* Grandma!"

"Why?" Morag asked curiously.

Peggy pursed up her lips, looking far older than her ten or eleven years. "You'll find out! She's all right with Daddy. She's even all right with Kimon. But if you're a *girl*, she's horrid!"

CHAPTER TWO

PERICLES took one look at his daughter's face and said something to her in Greek. The child looked gratified and smiled and nodded.

"Morag says she prefers being a girl," she said in English.

Pericles looked amused. His glance swept over Morag's heightened colour. "I expect she does," he agreed, his eyes inscrutable. "Give her back her necklace, Peggy. Being given that sort of thing is one of the perks –"

"She said I could have them!" Peggy protested.

"But I gave them to her," her father insisted quietly. "If you want another necklace yourself, I'll buy you another one. But that one was specially for Morag. Hand it over, there's a love!"

Peggy drew the shell necklace over her head and held it out with a reluctance that made Morag feel sympathetic. "It's true, I did give it to her. I can buy another necklace for myself. I'll go and find the boy –"

"No, you won't," Pericles muttered. He held her firmly by the wrist, still smiling. Morag wasn't even sure that he knew how tightly his grasp was, or even that he was touching her at all. "That necklace was for you. Those frightful plastic beads that spoil the shells go with the colour of your eyes. It was the only one he had with green beads and those pretty, curving shells, and you're going to keep it. If Peggy's isn't as nice, it's her own fault. No one else broke the one she had."

"I didn't get one at all!" Kimon complained in an aggrieved voice.

"You aren't a girl!" Peggy retorted, somewhat smugly. "Only girls get necklaces."

"Grandma will give me something else," Kimon answered, completely put out.

Peggy gave Morag a speaking look that told its own story. Morag looked straight back at her. "I'd rather have my shells," she said with a firmness that surprised even herself.

"Grandma will give me a coin for my collection!" Kimon went on belligerently.

"I don't care!" Peggy decided.

Morag smiled at her and the child smiled cheerfully back.

"What is this?" Pericles asked. "Feminine collusion? A fine thing! Kimon and I will have to watch out to see that you don't get the better of us!"

Peggy blinked. "Not of you, Daddy," she said carefully, "but it will be nice to get the better of Grandma. She's *always* giving Kimon things, and it isn't fair. Morag will be on my side!"

"Is that so?" her father drawled. "Grandma does her best for you, Peggy. You need a woman on hand when you're growing up —"

"Then I choose Morag. I *like* Morag!"

"But I can't be there all the time," Morag said, embarrassed.

"Why not?" said Peggy. "Why can't she stay with us, Daddy?"

Pericles shrugged his shoulders. "Why not?" he echoed. "Let's kidnap her and take her home with us —"

"And keep her for ever and ever!" Peggy finished for him.

"Yes," agreed Kimon. "I'd like that too."

"But not for *ever*!" Morag said firmly. "I *can't* stay for ever. I have to go back to England at the end of the holidays."

"Why?" said Pericles.

"Why?" said Kimon and Peggy in unison.

Morag's eyes widened as she faced the three of them. Why not indeed? What was to stop her? "I have my own

23

family," she began, sounding so unconvinced that Pericles laughed.

"You have now," he murmured, and, sweeping aside any further objections she might have, he went on, "The Holmes family – at least for a while, until you're quite sure that you don't want us any more."

And that was likely to be never, she thought in a bemused way. Her heart had always been far too swift to love and to hate, and she knew herself to be helplessly enmeshed with this family despite only just having met them. They seemed familiar to her, as if she had known them for years instead of minutes. Besides, there was the strange elation she felt whenever she looked at Pericles – an emotion she had never experienced before and which she didn't know now how to handle. It was a far remove from the quiet devotion she had felt for David, if devotion it had been. Perhaps he had been no more than a handy receptacle for her to pour her feelings into, and neither of them had really loved each other. She gave Pericles an oblique look from under her lashes and wondered what it would be like to be loved by him. It was a thought that couldn't help but dismay her.

Her feelings must have shown clearly on her face, for he laughed suddenly and said, "You'd already decided to come with us, remember? I'm not going to let you get out of it now!"

He opened the door of the car for her and pushed her on to the seat with a rough gallantry that brought a smile to her lips.

"Where does your mother live?" she asked.

"Lagonissi. It's on the Apollon coast, on the way to Sounion. She used to live in Glyfada, but when they developed the international airport there, she found the noise a bit much and moved a bit further out of Athens. It's mostly hotels and tourist apartments and villas, and it's quite near where the President has his villa. The swimming is good, but the life is a bit unreal."

"You don't care for it very much?" she hazarded.

"No, my dear, I do not. But I can't persuade my mother to move, and as the object of the exercise was for us to live with her, we were landed with it." He gave her an amused look. "With your advent, if you last, we may find somewhere else for ourselves and leave my poor mother in peace."

"Oh yes, please, Daddy," the children exhorted him.

"You can see why my mother doesn't enjoy their company much," he added dryly. "They have a distressing honesty –"

"Is that bad?" she interrupted him.

"Not when mixed with a rudiment of good manners, but it can be rather devastating when naked and unadorned!"

Morag laughed, "I can imagine!"

His mouth twitched. "I suppose you've seen the results of a like honesty yourself, being the same sort of person?" he said.

"Am I?" She was surprised first and then nettled. "I rather pride myself on my manners!" she objected.

"I'll remind you of that when you've coped with all three of us yelling at one another. We try to keep to a laid down pecking order. The children can yell at each other, you can yell at them, and I yell at you! Okay?"

"Do we have to yell at all?" she countered. She wasn't sure that she liked the idea of being yelled at by him.

"There's nothing wrong with your lungs, is there?" he asked with pretended concern. "We all yell, Morag. Perhaps you never yelled enough as a child."

"It wasn't the approved method of expression!"

"How forbidding you sound," he teased her. "I didn't know you were ever so disapproving!"

She lifted her chin. "But then you don't know me at all, Mr. Holmes!"

"You can call me Perry, if you like," he invited her.

"I don't like!"

"Then you'd better make it Pericles."

"I don't like that either!"

He grinned, "You'll get used to it." He touched her cheek with his finger and shut the door on her. "You're beginning to yell quite nicely," he added. "Only you're not allowed to yell at me. You're only allowed to yell at the children."

Morag was silent the whole way through Athens. She found the traffic nerve-racking and was ashamed of her fears, for Pericles drove both carefully and well. He even seemed to know where he was going, up and down the one-way streets, but then she supposed he had made the journey many times. For a while she wondered why the waiting cars invariably hooted when the traffic lights changed from red to green, but then she realised that they were almost impossible to see from those in front, and amused herself by trying to will Pericles forward before anyone had time to hoot at him. She was not sorry, though, when they had finally driven through the city, passing close beneath the cream-coloured Acropolis, surely the finest monument that any city can boast as its central feature, and came out at last on to the coast road.

"Not far now," Pericles smiled at her.

She relaxed a little in her seat. "They drive very fast, don't they?" she said, annoyed by the note of apology in her voice.

"It seems faster to the uninitiated. It's a bit baffling at first, finding one's way round the city. Looking at a map doesn't help much, unless the one-way systems are marked. You'll soon learn them."

"I don't drive!" The sharpness of her tone made her bite her lip. "I mean, I can't just now."

"Banned as well as fined? It might be as well if you kept that item of information from my mother, Morag."

"I don't think I'd drive in Greece anyway," she said

defiantly. "I'm not a very experienced driver. My father doesn't like women driving his car, and I haven't one of my own."

Pericles smiled faintly. "My mother expects all young people to drive, especially young English women. If you say you don't drive, it may even be a point in your favour. Susan didn't drive either."

"Your wife?"

He nodded. "Susan was brought up in Greece in a rather old-fashioned household. Women here are taught to obey their husbands and to leave all the decisions to them. Before that, they obey their fathers and learn all the domestic arts. Driving a car isn't often included in their education."

"Oh," said Morag.

"Is that all you have to say? I thought you'd start yelling at me again about the equality of women in modern society –"

Morag laughed. "A bit obvious, Mr. Holmes!"

"Pericles."

"Mr. Holmes," she said again, "I told you, I prefer Mr. Holmes."

"Morag –"

"Yes, Mr. Holmes?"

"There's a Greek side to my nature that prefers women to be meek and obedient. I don't expect to have to repeat myself when I give you an order. You are to call me Pericles. Understood?"

She nodded. It occurred to her that she was a little afraid of Pericles Holmes and that she didn't entirely dislike the sensation. "I suppose it would be silly as you call me Morag," she managed. It was not much of a last word, but it was the best that she could manage under the circumstances.

"I am in a privileged position," he said with a sardonic smile. "I'll call you anything I please."

"Isn't that rather unfair?"

"Life is unfair," he said.

He turned off the main coastal road shortly after that, apparently heading straight into the sea. "Welcome to my mother's house," he said formally. "Kimon, you can make yourself useful by carrying Morag's knapsack inside. That's one of the other perks that we allow the girls."

"Kimon doesn't carry my things for me," Peggy said at once.

"I do that!" her father reminded her. "Who's carrying your necklace now?"

"Morag. You only carry heavy things."

Morag giggled unexpectedly. "I'm sure a Greek man wouldn't do that!" she said. "I thought it was the women who did all the work!"

"Would that they did!" he returned drily. He smiled slowly at her. "You look quite pretty when you're amused," he told her. "We'll have to have you laughing more often."

She shook her head, her cheeks hot. "I'll never be pretty."

He touched her on the cheek, flicking her nose with one finger. "You're right, pretty is the wrong word, but I could find you very attractive, Morag Grant, if you smiled a little more."

She tried to pass it off as casually as he had made the remark. "Then I'll have to be as sober as a judge," she said, and if her voice trembled she was almost sure that only she had noticed it.

"You can try!" he said.

"I – I –" She swallowed. "David –" she began hesitantly.

He lifted his eyebrows in mute enquiry. "Yes?" he prompted her when she still said nothing.

"David thought I was pretty – sometimes."

He shook his head at her. "Morag! And that was enough
28

to make you love him?" He put a hand under her chin and forced her to look up at him. She tried to back away, but the warmth in his eyes stopped her. "You don't know what love means, do you? When it does come to you, fretting after what might have been with David will seem a poor substitute for the real thing. You don't owe him anything." He touched her cheek again, half-smiling. "Come in and meet my mother. She'll be very glad to see you, I promise you. She hasn't found it easy having the children here, any more than they have enjoyed being with her. Are you ready?"

She nodded, unable to find any words in which to answer him. She put up her hand to her cheek where he had touched her, wondering at the weakness which assailed her. She would have to pull herself together before she met his mother. What would *she* think if her unknown guest was quite incapable of greeting her in anything other than a foolish monosyllable, just because – because *what*?

Morag had no time to do more than brush down her tight-fitting jeans and try to smooth her shirt that, what with the heat and the dust from the day, was scarcely looking as neat and fresh as when she had put it on in the morning. Pericles drew her inexorably into the house after him and out again on to the verandah on the other side. He let go of her there, bending over the elegant figure of the woman who sat, straight-backed, on a wooden chair, looking out towards the sea.

"You're home in time for the sunset tonight," Mrs. Holmes said. "I thought you might have gone to Sounion as the children have never seen our most famous local site – Poseidon's temple in the dying sun, when his famous blue hair turns to grey. Sometimes I can almost believe that he's real when I watch the sea taking on the colours of the heavens. That is why I love this house!"

Pericles kissed her lightly on the cheek. "I brought some-one home with me. She's going to give a hand with the children for the rest of the summer. Mama, this is Morag Grant."

His mother swivelled round in her chair, a look of shock on her face. "A *stranger*, Perry? How could you?"

"I think you may come to like her," he answered calmly.

"But what does she know of our Greek ways?"

"We're not wholly Greek," her son reminded her. "Besides, I think you'll find her willing to learn. She's very amenable." The amusement in his voice stung Morag into speech. She took a deep breath and held out a hand to the older woman.

"*Héro poli*," she said in Greek, hoping that she had got it right.

Pericles' mother favoured her with a long, searching look. "*Miláte Elliniká?*" she enquired, finally shaking hands.

"No," Morag admitted. "I tried to learn a few phrases before I came. It seems only civil to try and speak to people a few words of their own language, but most people seem to speak English, and I suppose I'm a bit lazy too."

"The children both speak excellent Greek," Kyria Holmes said. "It's my wish that they should converse as much as possible in their own language. We have decided that both their lives lie in this country and it is as well for them to learn how to be wholly Greek, whatever my son may say. Do you really think you can help us to achieve that purpose?"

"I can try," Morag answered her.

"No, no, it's impossible! Peggy especially needs to be taught that Greek women don't get their own way by throwing tantrums whenever they are crossed! When she grows up and marries, her husband will control her destiny, just as her father should be doing now. Wanting to do everything just the same as Kimon does will be of little use then!

Morag looked quickly at Pericles. "It this what you want for your daughter?"

30

"I'd like her to marry a strong man," he admitted. "As for the rest, I suppose it was the way her mother was brought up."

"Certainly it was!" his mother exclaimed.

Morag saw Pericles' lips tighten. "It might have been better for her if she'd shown more spirit," he remarked.

"I suppose you are referring to that foolish incident when she thought she was in love with Takis? Did she make you a less good wife because of that? Your slightest wish was her command right up until her death."

"Oh, quite!" he said.

Morag thought she detected an underlying bitterness in his words. "Who is Takis?" she asked, seeking to divert his attention from thoughts of his wife.

"Takis Kapandriti is my nephew." Kyria Holmes drew herself up. "He is staying with us at this moment. You will probably meet him sooner or later. He goes out a great deal as he has business in Athens."

Morag looked about her, suddenly wondering what her own position in the house was to be. "Is – is there room –"

Kyria Holmes rose to her feet. "It's a large house, Miss Grant. My son would not have brought you here otherwise." She nodded formally and went inside without a backward look, calling out to the children as she went.

Morag shrugged her shoulders.

Pericles looked amused. "She isn't really frightening once you get used to her," he reassured her. His face crinkled into a smile. "I think she was trying to warn you about Takis in her own way. Stay clear of him, Morag. He isn't going to marry for a long time yet and he might not understand that there are some English girls who don't come here for the one thing only. Our Greek women are very closely protected by their families and British freedoms are apt to be misunderstood."

"But I haven't even met him yet!" Morag protested.

31

"There's no harm in making things clear from the beginning," he observed drily. "Takis is never serious and you are not to encourage him. Is that clear?"

"What do you expect me to do? Ignore him completely?" She faced him angrily. "It may not be very Greek, Mr. Holmes, but I make my own decisions of that kind no matter where I am!"

"Not very successfully," he reminded her. "It won't hurt you, while you're here, to do things my way. It's time someone put the brakes on where you're concerned. You are obviously warm-hearted to a fault, but that can make for sloppiness if you're not careful. Takis would only take advantage of you – as easily as that David of yours, for instance."

She glared at him. "Thank you very much!" she stormed. "You don't know anything about it! How dare you –"

"Easily!"

"Well, you can stay out of my business once and for all! You can be as high-handed as you like with your own children, though I don't think you're at all fair to Peggy, but no one speaks like that to me!"

He actually chuckled. It was the last straw as far as she was concerned. "I *hate* you, Pericles Holmes!" she declared. "I'm going! I can't think why I ever came with you! *Goodbye!*"

He leaned against one of the verandah pillars, folding his arms across his chest.

"What a fuss!" he mocked her.

"You can't keep me here against my will!"

"No?"

The single syllable seemed doubly insulting to her; first because it implied she didn't know her own mind, and second because it held a threat that she wanted to challenge but didn't quite dare to put it to the test. She was afraid of Pericles Holmes, she thought, even while he attracted her.

32

"If I do stay," she began. "*If* I do, you must understand –"

"You'll stay," he said certainly.

Her lips quivered. "I won't be dictated to!"

"And I won't be yelled at by –"

"A mere woman, you mean?" she said easily. "I'll yell whenever I feel like it!"

"Not at me you won't!" He laughed suddenly. "I might have known your green eyes could flash with temper as much as any other emotion! But don't flash them at me, Morag Grant. You might get more of a reaction than you bargained for!"

She shrugged her shoulders, bitterly aware that she had somehow lost the battle and that he knew she had no intention of going anywhere. "Indeed?" was all she said.

"Indeed, *Kortsi mou.*"

She stood stock still, annoyed to find that she wanted to find out exactly what reaction she would inspire in him if she continued the argument. It was very tempting to her to find out. She gave him an uncertain look. "I'm not sloppy!"

His eyebrows rose. "All right," he said. "I take that back. You're not sloppy. You're just more feminine than is good for you." A mocking smile touched his lips. "But I won't tease you any more. It's too soon for you to know what you want for the future and you need to keep a tight hold on your heart without any commitments until you know which way you're looking. Only don't tempt me, Morag. I'm only a man, and making love to you wouldn't be at all disagreeable to me, especially when you look at me as though you expect me to pounce on you at any moment!"

"You forget," she said quietly, "it's not long since I lost my fiancé –"

He snapped his fingers, making an angry noise in his mouth. "Grow up, Morag! You didn't love David. He gave you a nice romantic feeling, no more than that! If I took you on, you'd find out what loving a man means. You

33

wouldn't cast me off on your sister when you're tired of me!"

Morag gaped at him. "I don't know what you're talking about!"

"Oh yes, you do! Do you think Delia, or whatever her name is, would have succeeded in interesting David if you hadn't half wanted it that way?"

"You don't know Delia."

"It's got nothing to do with Delia. I'm sure she is prettier than you, more attractive, more *everything*, but that wouldn't have resigned you to losing David to her. What if she has always taken everything she thought you wanted away from you? If you'd really wanted David you would have fought back, and you'd have gone on fighting until you had them both where you wanted them!"

Morag looked as surprised as she felt. "Would I?" she said. "I don't see how you could know that." Her eyes kindled with indignation. "If I wouldn't do it for David, I certainly wouldn't do it for you!"

Suddenly he took a step toward her and she panicked, almost running away from him to the far end of the verandah. "One day," he said, "I'll take you up on that, when you've had time to know me better."

An extraordinary, totally unfamiliar excitement ran through her. "You may have treated Susan to the masterful approach, but I shouldn't care for it at all!"

His laughter unsettled her badly. "Susan was well broken in long before she was chosen as a suitable wife for me. She obeyed, but she never loved, poor girl. They should have allowed her to marry Takis – she had more than enough money for them both! All I could do was to be gentle and to encourage her as far as possible to do things for herself. It was I who introduced her to the flying which finally killed her, but I don't regret it! At least it gave her a few moments of freedom from the quagmire in which she found herself."

The colour rose in Morag's cheeks and she veiled her

eyes from him, more than a little shy. "If you felt like that about her, why should you want –" She broke off, not wanting to put the threat she felt for him into words after all. She might have misunderstood him and then what would he think of her?

"To tame you?" His smile told her that he had read her thoughts exactly. "Perhaps because you'd revel in the battle as much as I. You're not like Susan in any way. She found marriage to me a prison, a comfortable prison for which she had been well prepared with a lifetime of submission to what her family decided was good for her. I was no more than her warder, carrying out the sentence they had passed on her. It would be different with you, Morag Grant. You would find freedom –"

She couldn't bear to hear any more. "Never with you!"

"Never with David!" he retorted. "Never with any man who wouldn't demand everything you have to give, who wouldn't make you wholly his – in every way!"

Morag swallowed. "I think that's a highly improper thing to say. I d–don't want to listen to you any more."

He strolled across the verandah towards her, stopping so close to her that they were almost touching. Her breath caught in the back of her throat and she was more afraid than ever, not so much of him as of herself.

"Improper?" he repeated. "Why? Because I haven't known you long enough? It doesn't take time for me to know I'd like to kiss you, or for you to know that you'd like me to! Shall I give you a practical demonstration, *karthia mou*?"

"*No!*" The negative exploded out of her.

"Another time?" He put a hand under her chin and forced her to look up at him. "Cheer up, sweetheart, I'll try not to rush you. You'll be quite safe with me." He stroked her cheek with a gentle finger, bringing the burning colour rushing in the wake of his touch. Then he bent his head and his lips met hers in a caress so fleeting that

35

she couldn't be sure that it had actually happened.

The sound of footsteps coming on to the verandah made him take a swift step away from her. "Damn!" he muttered under his breath. Morag showed him a shaken face and he smiled straight back at her. "Perhaps it's just as well," he murmured. "You have to meet Takis some time, and now is as good a time as any."

She had no time to say anything at all. Takis came out on to the verandah and stopped, blinking at them. He was a whole head shorter than his cousin, but he looked far less Greek. His hair was fair and his eyes were pale grey and rather hard.

"Thia Dora said we had a guest." His lips parted in a smile. "Has she something in her eye, or am I interrupting something?"

"Neither," Pericles said shortly. "Morag, this is my cousin Takis. Takis, Morag Grant. She's going to help with the children."

Takis took her hand in his and raised it to his lips. He smiled and winked at Morag, sharing with her the knowledge that he knew he was annoying his cousin by his too gallant greeting of her. Morag gave him back look for look and found herself smiling despite herself. Really, it was too ridiculous, but Takis Kapandriti was more like David than anyone else she had ever met!

CHAPTER THREE

TAKIS seldom actually went into the water. He preferred
to stand close to where the sea lapped gently at the shore,
filling his lungs with the golden air and showing off his
fine golden body to their neighbours.

"A few weeks and you'll have a fine tan yourself,"
he said to Morag, his eyes openly approving her neat
figure. "Shall I put some oil on your back for you before
you burn?"

"No, thank you."

"So shy! But you are not shy with my cousin Pericles,
are you? Now why do you favour him, I wonder? You
would do much better with me, little *anglitha*. I haven't
two children and a second-hand love to offer you!"

Morag's eyes flashed. "Certainly not second-hand!" she
murmured.

"What do you mean by that?" he demanded.

"What you think! You've scarcely been out with the
same girl twice since I've been here!"

"Does that offend you? But they are not serious girls,
Morag. They are only to have fun with, you understand."

Morag shut her eyes, wriggling her shoulders into a more
comfortable position. "I used to know someone very like
you," she remarked.

"And that is why you don't like me?" he reproached her.

"I do like you. I liked him too – very much!"

"Ah!" She felt his shadow come between herself and the
sun. "Tell me about this interesting man you used to
know!"

"There's nothing to tell."

"*Nothing?*"

37

"He's dead now, and you remind me of him. That's all there is to it."

"He must have been a fine man!" Takis exclaimed, naïve with self-pride. "How long did you know him?"

Morag hesitated. "He was a friend of my family," she said at last.

"You were in love with him?"

"I thought I was for a little while. But he wasn't ready to love anyone, and I wasn't either. Just like you!"

"I am offended!" Takis told her. "You imply that I am childish. I'm not, not at all. There is nothing childish in liking women, is there?"

"No," said Morag.

"Then why do you imply that I am childish?"

"You don't like responsibilities."

"I like you," he said slyly.

She ignored that. She remembered that David had complained that she had thought him indecisive and how much he had resented her implied criticism of him. She had felt old in his company, older than he, just as she did with Takis. She turned her back on him, trying to still her sudden swift heartbeat as she reflected that Pericles didn't have that effect on her at all.

"Why do you do that?" Takis demanded. "I like to talk with you!"

"The sun's too hot and I'm too sleepy," she answered. "Besides, the children will be home in a minute."

"All the more reason to make the best use of this minute," he said with a laugh. He put his hand on her back and stroked her shoulders. "I told you you needed some oil. You are red now. When the sun goes down it will be very painful. Shall I put some oil on for you now?"

"I'd rather you didn't."

"Why not? It will be nice for you. You can shut your eyes and pretend it is this man you once loved who is doing this for you. It will make you happy and then you won't burn."

38

Morag gave him a determined look. "I don't want –" she began.

He smiled the smile that was so like David's, that touched his lips but never quite reached his cold, grey eyes. It was funny that she had only noticed that about David in the last few weeks she had known him.

"You will have a sore back otherwise," he reiterated. He put some oil in the palm of his hand and began to smooth it on to her back. "Isn't that nice?"

"It will probably come up in blisters!"

"No, no, my touch will prevent all such disasters. I have a very nice touch, *ne*?" He spilt some more oil straight on to her back and drew patterns in it with one finger. "Your hair is in the way. You have pretty hair. I like it." He pushed it away from her shoulders and, a second later, she felt his lips on the back of her neck and turned indignantly towards him. "Ah, that is much better!" he said at once. "You like it? You like it very much!"

"I won't have it!" she said hotly. "Go away, Takis, and leave me alone!"

"But you like it! I am handsome and I know very well how to treat a girl! Why should you wish me to leave you alone?"

"Because I don't like playing at love –"

"Only with Pericles!"

"Not with anyone!" she said. "I look after Pericles' children, nothing more!"

"That wasn't how it seemed the first time I saw you. Why do you dislike me? I am more handsome than Pericles. It is known that women prefer me to him!"

Morag jumped to her feet. "You're more conceited too!" she said.

He grinned up at her. "I say only the truth! Even his wife, Susan, preferred me to him. Oh, she was very much in love with me! But her father said she must marry Pericles –"

"I don't want to hear about it!"

39

He stood up also. "I think you do. I think you are very curious about the woman Pericles married, the mother of his children. Are you jealous of her?"

"Why should I be?" Morag demanded.

"Because she knew both of us well. Shall I kiss you like I used to kiss her?"

"I don't believe you did kiss her!" Morag said, but there was no conviction in her words.

"Oh yes, I kissed her – before she was married, I kissed her. Afterwards, she would not be alone with me. Pericles forbade it and Susan was a very dutiful wife. But we both knew that she wanted to be with me, and Pericles knew it too!"

"I suppose you saw to that!" Morag said coldly. "You must enjoy hurting people to relish a thing like that!"

"But I don't wish to hurt you!" he claimed. "I want only for you to have fun with me. What's wrong with that?"

"Go away!"

"When you tell me why I must not kiss you. You see, you cannot! You will like it very much, my little English girl!" He tried to suit the action to his words, holding her tight against him and smothering her face with kisses, but Morag, lent strength by her own fury, pulled herself free and walked away from him across the beach towards the house.

Takis ran along behind her. "You have a heart like a stone!" he accused her. "You look like a pretty woman, but you have no feelings, or you would show me that you like me a little."

"I don't like you at all!" Morag retorted.

"I shall make you like me!"

"Oh no, not that again!" she said desperately. But she was too late. He caught her to him and tried to kiss her again, taking no notice of her efforts to free herself from his restricting hands.

"*Takis!*"

The bruising grip of his fingers relaxed and Morag tore herself away from him only to find herself face to face with Pericles.

"It wasn't my fault," she said.

"The children are home," was all he said. "Go up to the house and see to them."

"Yes, Mr. Holmes."

"And, Miss Grant –" he added.

She turned towards him. "Yes?"

"I think it was your fault. I told you to stay away from my cousin."

"But he doesn't mean any harm, Perry!"

"How do you know that?" He bit out the words, strong angry lines etching themselves on to his face. "How can you possibly know that?"

"He's like David. He has to show off. His beauty is all he has!"

Pericles' face softened a little. "How like David? Enough for you to fall for his feckless brand of charm?"

She shook her head. "I'll go and see to the children." She wished she had something more to cover herself with than the towel she had brought with her to the beach. Takis had looked at her with an open admiration and she had hardly noticed, but Pericles had only to allow his eyes to drop to the smocked top of her swimming-suit and she felt half-naked and shamed by the fact that she was vulnerable to his slightest change of mood.

He nodded shortly. "I'll speak to you later. If Takis is annoying you, I'll do something about it. But I won't have you encouraging him, Morag, no matter how like David he is! It's time you faced facts and grew up a little!"

She was determined not to cry. That would have been the final humiliation. But it was hard not to cavil at the injustice of that last remark. How could he think she would encourage Takis when – yes, it might as well be said – when *he* was living in the same house and when she

41

couldn't think about anything or anyone else when he was around? She *had* faced facts, at least she had faced the only fact that mattered, and that was that she was more than a little in love with Pericles Holmes. The trouble was that she had thought, that first evening, that he had found her a little special too, but he had given no further sign that he liked her.

"I'm sorry," she said.

"You'll be more than sorry if I catch you flirting with him again!" he told her grimly.

"It wasn't my fault!" she declared again. The tears spilled over and ran down her cheeks and she brushed them away with an impatient hand. "I don't even like him!"

His eyes glinted as they caught the sun. "Remember that!" he advised her. "And stay away from him!"

She climbed the steps that had been cut into the rock leading up to the villa, doing her best to control her tears. She would not cry! She rubbed her face in her towel and tripped over a loose piece of stone, falling heavily against the rough side of the steps. The pain of the graze down the side of her leg put her tears to flight, but she felt that somehow that too was all Pericles' fault and that it wouldn't have happened if he had spoken to her more kindly.

"Morag, Morag, are you hurt?"

She looked up from her leg to smile at Kimon's anxious face. "I'll live," she told him. "It isn't very bad."

"You weren't looking where you were going," he rebuked her. He took a deep breath. "Did Daddy tell you?"

"Tell me what?"

Kimon frowned. For him, there was only one important matter on foot at the moment. He hugged himself with glee, jumping up and down. "Did he tell you what Grandma has given me? Did he? It's the most gorgeous thing you've ever seen. Can you guess what it is?"

Morag considered the matter. "A new fishing rod," she hazarded. She knew that Kimon had wanted one ever since he had come to Greece.

"No! That's quite *ordinary*! This is special!"

"I don't know," Morag said. "You'll have to tell me."

"It's a Spartan coin. You know, one of their iron cart-wheels. It's terrific! All the other Greeks used to laugh at them because they wouldn't make their coins smaller and easier to handle, like the Athenians did. But the Spartans were the toughest people in the world and they didn't mind if their money did wear out their clothing. They seldom carried it around anyway. Do you want to see it? It's just like those you can see in the musuem."

Morag was caught up in his enthusiasm. "I'd love to. I didn't know you were interested in coins," she added as Kimon ran ahead of her towards the house.

"Oh yes, I've collected them for ages!"

Morag allowed herself to be hauled off into his room. "What about Peggy?" she asked. "What does she collect?"

"Girls don't collect things," he declared. "She used to like collecting different pebbles and stones, but Grandma said they were rubbish and made her throw them away."

"I used to collect stamps," Morag remembered.

"Did you?" He was diverted for an instant from getting his precious coin out of its hiding place at the back of his drawer. "Peggy used to polish her stones. They were quite pretty. But it doesn't do for a girl to get interested in men's things – they have to do other things."

"Can't they do both?" Morag asked innocently.

The boy shrugged. "Grandma doesn't think so," he answered. "When she was young, she wanted to paint more than anything. She used to do the most marvellous pictures, but my grandfather painted too and his paintings had to be better. He made Grandma destroy all hers when she married him. She says it's much better not to get to like doing things if you can't go on with them."

"Your grandfather sounds like a bigoted old man to me!" Morag observed dryly.

43

Kimon grinned. "That's what Daddy says to Grandma when she goes on about Peggy. Look, don't you think it's the nicest coin you've ever seen?"

Morag did. She put the wheel-shaped coin on the palm of her hand and twisted it this way and that, marvelling at the age of such a piece and the workmanship that allowed the spokes-like pattern to be seen so many hundreds of years later.

"What did Peggy get?" she asked.

Kimon had the grace to look a bit guilty. "Grandma didn't give her anything," he admitted. "Peggy doesn't mind!"

"I'm afraid she does," Morag said, returning the coin. "I think she minds very much."

Kimon thought for a moment. "Peggy will get a dowry when she marries," he pointed out. "She'll have a house and all sorts of things!" He put his precious coin back in his drawer. "She won't get married if she doesn't. Well, I suppose she might, to someone in Athens or one of the big cities, but not to an islander or someone more old-fashioned. Have you got a dowry?"

"No," said Morag.

"Mummy had one. Grandma says she brought a great deal into the family."

Morag pursed her lips together thoughtfully. "I think I'll give Peggy something. What do you think she'd like?"

Kimon went pink. "Have you still got your stamps?" he asked. "She'd like that. I thought I'd give her my scout-knife, but Grandma would only take it away from her. But she needn't know about the stamps!"

"They're in England," Morag said, feeling rather guilty that she should encourage the children to have secrets from their grandmother. "I could ask my stepmother to send them, I suppose."

"And meanwhile you could tell Peggy about them! Have you got many?"

44

"Not very many. But I've got some very nice ones. A few pretty ones from Africa, and a few quite valuable ones from all over the Commonwealth."

"You could tell her about those," Kimon enthused. "Peggy likes to know what things are worth."

Like her grandmother! But it wasn't fair that Kimon should receive so many valuable gifts and Peggy none at all. "You can tell her about the stamps, if you want to, Kimon," she said aloud.

"May I? She'll be thrilled to bits!"

He pushed past her with a whoop of joy, shouting for his sister as he went. Morag smiled after him. If everyone were so easy to please, how simple life would be!

Kyria Holmes barely looked up as Morag came into the room. "What is all the noise about?" she asked in her heavily accented English.

"Kimon was showing me his coin."

Kyria Holmes sniffed. "I fail to see why it should involve so much noise. You have little control over the children, although that is supposed to be the reason why you are here. I have told Pericles that I think it would be a mistake to allow them to become too fond of you. Children should be kept at a distance, Miss Grant, not made the centre of things."

Morag stiffened. "I don't agree, *kyria*."

"Why not?"

Morag was astonished by the question. She had thought the older woman would merely have snubbed her for giving her unasked opinion, but then Pericles' mother seldom did the thing which was expected of her.

"I think children should be encouraged to be confident and sure of themselves," she answered. "No one should think less of themselves than the best."

"That is a very Greek sentiment," the Kyria said mildly. "It is all right for men, but it's harder when one is a woman.

45

I would like to have been born a man! I would have shown the world –" She broke off, biting her lip. "I'm told you prefer being a woman, Miss Grant. Peggy says that you claim you have more fun as a girl. I find it unbelievable, but perhaps you have never wanted to do anything very much and then found you can't?"

"No, I haven't," Morag admitted.

"Then you don't know what you're talking about!"

"I suppose not, but if I wanted to do something very much, I'd do it!" She licked her lips, a little afraid of what she was about to say. "*Kyria*, why don't you start painting again?"

The silence stretched interminably between them, then the Kyria said: "Pericles would not permit it!"

"What's it got to do with him?" The words were out before she could stop them, but Morag could not bring herself to regret them.

Kyria Holmes merely stared at her. "He is my son!"

"But he wouldn't stop you painting. Why should he?"

"His father didn't approve of my work. Pericles would think it disloyal of me if I were to start again now!"

"I've never heard anything so ridiculous!" Morag exploded. "I'll ask him! I'm not afraid of him, if you are!"

To her surprise, the older woman laughed. "Young people these days are afraid of nothing. But I think you are not quite so casual in the way you treat my son as you pretend, no?"

Morag coloured faintly. "What makes you say that?"

"You are very brave on my behalf, but would you defy Pericles for yourself? I think not, my dear. You are not so different from your Greek sisters after all. You seek the approval of the man who controls your life, and that is good, very good – "

"Pericles doesn't control my life!" Morag said.

"Does your father?"

"No one does!"

Kyria Holmes gave a superior smile. "The new, liberated woman? My dear, how little you know about yourself. In England, when my husband was alive, I met many of them and they were none of them like you!"

Morag chewed on her lip, not enjoying the turn the conversation had taken. "Anyway," she said, "we were talking about you. Why don't you paint again?"

"You don't believe me about Pericles?"

Morag opened her eyes wide. "No."

"He is not my husband, it is true. Pericles would not stop me painting if he knew I wanted to do so, but I'm afraid that after all this time I'd be no good. Worse still, I might not know that I was no good. Do you understand me? My husband refused to allow me to paint on principle. Women, he said, could never be better than second-rate in the arts. I could not disobey him, so I did as he asked and destroyed my paintings, but not the desire, never the urge to paint!"

Morag wondered why, if she felt like that, she should seek to impose the same rigid ideas on women on her granddaughter, but then she didn't begin to understand what moved the older woman – perhaps Pericles did.

"Pericles would want you to try," she said certainly.

Kyria Holmes looked amused. "Thank you, my dear. I will ask my son when he comes in."

"Ask me what?" Pericles said from the doorway. His eyes were on Morag and she was very conscious of his gaze.

"Morag – Miss Grant – "

"I think you should get used to calling her Morag, Mama."

His mother lifted her eyebrows, but she said nothing. "Morag has been trying to persuade me to start painting again. What do you think of that?" She threw back her head, challenging her son to renege on his father's ban. "She has impertinence, this young English girl!"

"Very impertinent," Pericles agreed. Morag looked up

47

quickly and saw that he was smiling. "And a revolutionary in her own way. Peggy is jumping over the moon because she is going to collect stamps – yes, Mama, she is. *I* have told her that she may! – and now here you are, all set to start painting again!"

His mother compressed her lips. "I have changed my mind!"

"Because you don't want to be grateful to Morag?"

Morag was shocked that he should suggest such a thing. "She's afraid, Perry. Besides, why should she be grateful to me —"

"I'm not!" Kyria Holmes assured her. "To suggest that I am afraid!" She tossed her head. "If Pericles says I may start painting again then I shall do so!"

"I'll buy some you paints next time I go to Athens," he promised.

His mother was far from pleased. "I shall buy my own paints! Afraid! Why should I be afraid of my own son?" She gave Morag a look filled with malicious amusement. "If anyone is afraid, Morag Grant, it is you, and well you might be if you always behave so freely with young men as you did with Takis on the beach. If you were my daughter, you would spend the rest of the evening in your room to teach you to be more circumspect! Such a sight! I'll leave you alone with Pericles and you can explain to him what you were doing!" She rapped Morag sharply over the knuckles with her open hand. "And then tell me you're not afraid of him!" she added in a low fierce whisper, and laughed a laugh so like her son's that Morag could only stare at her, hoping that Pericles hadn't heard her.

But Pericles had. One look at the mocking expression on his face was enough to convince her of that!

"I – I think your mother would be much happier if she could paint again!"

"Yes, I think she might be."

"And Peggy neeeds to collect something. If she can't

48

collect stones there isn't any reason why she shouldn't collect stamps, is there?"

"None at all."

"Then you don't mind?" she pressed him.

"Did you think I would?"

"N–no."

He came and sat down beside her. "Are you afraid of me, Morag?

She looked away from him. "Of course not!" The colour rose in her cheeks. "Your - your mother thinks that all women should be afraid of some man. But I am not! Why should I be?"

He sat back thrusting his legs out in front of him, looking the picture of ease and comfort. "Why are you?" he countered softly.

"I'm not – not really! I mean, it doesn't matter to me what you think of me. I don't have to stay here!"

She sought in vain for some kind of answer. "I don't know!" She threaded her fingers together, giving vent to her feelings in the only way she could think of. "I-I'm n-not!" she asserted.

His hand closed over hers. "Not at all?" She could feel his amusement and wondered why he could be so heartless.

"Why should I be?" she compromised.

"My mother is not unobservant," he remarked. He gave her a humorous look. "She likes you, did you know that?"

"She has a strange way of showing it! She needn't have mentioned Takis at all!"

He laughed and put an arm round her shoulders, pulling her close to him. "If she hadn't, I would have done. What did you mean, he's like David?"

She tried to ignore the feel of his arm about her, but it was hard when she could hardly breathe, let alone move, in case he should take it away again.

"He looks like David when he smiles," she said.

49

He was silent for a long moment, then he said, "Morag, will you marry me?"

Her heart pounded painfully against her ribs. She struggled upwards, but his arm pulled her back against him. "Why?" she whispered.

"You can't marry David – and I don't suppose Takis will oblige – "

"Why should I want to marry Takis?" she burst out. "I didn't want him to – to try to kiss me! I only meant that he likes to be admired and David did too! He couldn't bear it if people ignored him."

"Yet you loved him?"

She struggled with her conscience, more than half decided to lie to him. "I – I thought I did. I don't think I know very much above love. He was nice, though, Perry, and very handsome – just like Takis!"

"I see," he said.

"No, you don't! I thought nothing mattered when he was dead. Nothing *did* matter!" She bit her lip. "I like it here. I don't want to go home. They were glad when I left. They didn't say so, of course. They didn't have to! David would have taken me away from them – "

"Then stay here and marry me," Pericles murmured.

"But why should you want to? Kimon and Peggy – "

"Exactly," he said. "I've never seen Peggy happier than since you came here, and Kimon is more thoughtful of her feelings. They both love you, Morag, and I think they need you. Would that be enough for you?"

It wasn't, but she could hardly say so. How could she begin to explain that she wanted his love too? She shut her eyes and tried to imagine what it would be like if the arm that held her would tighten – and if he should kiss her, just the once, as if he meant it.

"Yes, it would be enough," she said. "But I'd stay anyway. You don't have to marry me. I'll stay as long as you want me!"

He put up his hand and pulled on the lobe of her ear, much as he might have done to Peggy. "Oh, Morag! Generous as ever, with never a thought for yourself!"

"Sloppy, don't you mean?"

"It's rather a nice characteristic when not taken to excess. If you marry me, there will be no more regrets for David, and no more romantic incidents with Takis. You will be my wife, do you understand that? In Greece, we take these things very seriously – "

"But don't you want to marry someone you love?" He deserved so much better, she thought. First Susan whom his family had chosen for him, and now herself because his children liked her!

"What about you?" He turned the question.

She took a deep breath. "I want to marry you," she said.

CHAPTER FOUR

Morag found saying goodbye to the children almost unbearable. "I suppose we have to go to England?" she said to Pericles.

"I think so. Your family will expect to see you safely married to me. It will only be a week before we're back here. It isn't very long."

"I know," she said. "But I wish we could be married here."

"I don't think my mother would thank you for the suggestion. All that trouble and fuss for an English girl she scarcely knows!"

Morag managed a smile. "I thinks she likes to embarrass me."

"You'll get used to it!"

Morag wasn't so sure. She found it difficult enough to come to terms with the idea of being Pericles' wife without her future mother-in-law's comments as to how her son would treat her once the ring was safely on her finger. Not that Morag believed that Perry was likely to beat her, or starve her, or even row with her in front of his family, but he was half Greek and the Greeks expected their wives to be subservient to them, and who knew which half of his blood dominated in Pericles? He might be as Greek in that as his name!

Pericles looked at her doubtful face and laughed. "Don't you want to introduce me to your family?" he asked curiously.

She was immediately enthusiastic. "Oh yes!" A flash of amusement entered her eye. "I shall very much enjoy showing you off to them. You're much better than anything that Delia has been able to produce!" Her expression clouded over for an instant. "You don't mind, do you? You'll probably like her," she added stiffly. "Most men do!"

"I hope I shall too," he drawled.

Morag felt despair round her heart. Delia would take one look at him and she would want him as surely as she had wanted anything else of Morag's, as she had wanted David. Well, she had taken David and Morag had cared, but she had not broken her heart over it, though for a time she had thought she had. But supposing Delia were to take Pericles from her? He was bound to find her beautiful and attentive and far, far more sophisticated than Morag could ever be. He was bound to prefer her to herself. It went without saying, and it was the one thing that she couldn't bear to happen. Pericles might not love her, but somehow or other he had stolen her heart from her, and that was the only reason she was marrying him, though she had agreed with every one of the practical reasons he had suggested to her, beginning with the children and ending with her own broken romance and the penalty the courts had imposed on her when she had taken responsibility for David's death and the corresponding gossip that had so dismayed her family. What else could she do but agree with him when he hadn't mentioned the word 'love' once to her certain knowledge?

"Pericles," she began. Her lashes swept down to hide her eyes.

"Uh-huh?"

"I wouldn't ask you to pretend exactly, but –" her cheeks turned scarlet. "I haven't told them that you find it convenient to marry me, because of the children and so on. Would you – would you mind very much – " She broke off, unable to continue.

"If I laid more stress on 'and so on' than on the children?" he suggested. There was amusement in his voice.

She didn't dare look at him. "They all knew that David

preferred Delia to me. We all pretended for a while, but they knew, just as I knew."

"Perhaps we should get into practice," he suggested.

Her eyes widened and she shot him a swift glance. The brilliant laughter in his eyes did nothing to reassure her. "I only meant," she said hurriedly, "that – that I'd prefer them to think that we were getting married for all the usual reasons – "

"I know exactly what you want them to think!" he said. "All right, *Karthia mou*, we'll play it your way. I may enjoy stringing them all along – especially Delia!" He put a hand beneath her hair on the nape of her neck and drew her towards him. She felt a suffocating sense of excitement and was immediately afraid that he would know how he affected her.

With a little gasp, she pulled away, but he would have none of it.

"You have to pay for your pride," she heard him say as from a distance. "We can't have you getting in a panic every time I touch you or no one will believe I find you irresistible, or that you melt with desire every time I come near you. That wouldn't do at all, would it?"

She licked her lips. "No," she said.

The pressure increased on the nape of her neck and, perforce, she had to take another step closer to him. His body was hard against hers and his arms were like two steel bands holding her tightly to him. The excitement within her exploded into something she had never experienced before. She was trembling and she scarcely knew whether it was with fear of the unknown, or with sheer longing for him to initiate her into that unknown.

"You're a better actress than I thought," he said dryly, pushing her hair back from her face. "I could swear you were enjoying this!"

She hid her face against his neck and pretended not to have heard him. But she could feel his laughter and it made

54

her tremble still more.

"Look up, little Morag," he said more gently. "How can I kiss you when you hide from me?"

She wished she had the courage to do as he asked, but she knew that if she did look up he would see what lay in her eyes.

His fingers stroked the nape of her neck for a few more seconds, then they entangled themselves in her hair and forced her head backwards whether she would or would not. She shut her eyes, putting her hands flat against his chest, her body tense and waiting. "You have to kiss me too, you know!"

"I can't," she breathed.

"Why not?" he touched her mouth lightly with his own. "You have two excellent lips just made for kissing. All you have to do is this and this – and *this*!" The first two kisses were meant to tease her, but the third was of a different quality. It began just like the others, but soon the pressure of his firm mouth parted her lips beneath his and she felt his male joy in conquest as her resistance flared and died, changing into a delicious surrender that wanted only to please him. Her arms slipped up behind his head and the tension went out of her. She felt his hands exploring her back and the soft curve of her breasts and she dug her fingers deeper into his hair. It was tough and virile like him and showed as little sign of bending to her will, and somehow, that pleased her too.

"*Yinéka*, for someone who can't kiss, you certainly would have fooled me!"

She took a deep breath, struggling to maintain a modicum of dignity. "Don't call me Greek names! I don't know what they mean!" She longed to fling herself back into his arms, to plead with him to kiss her again, but she knew that she couldn't do that.

"I'll call you any names I please," he said, the mockery back in his voice.

55

She blinked. "I wouldn't mind in English." She bit her lip, thinking that sounded craven. "Perry, I never – never kissed anyone like that before – "

"I should hope not!" he cut her off.

"I didn't know – "

He stopped her words with his mouth. "Hush, I know that too, Morag, I know it all!"

"How can you?" she wondered.

He kissed her hard and put her away from him, giving her a little push, even while he smiled at her. "Freedom is more dearly bought, sweetheart. That paid for your pride as far as your family is concerned. The payment I set on mine will ask more of you than that!"

"I don't understand," she said.

"You will!" he retorted, and she couldn't tell whether he meant it as a threat or a promise.

She bent her head. "I'll try to be a good wife to you." She thought perhaps his silence meant that he wasn't convinced. "I l-liked it just now – when you kissed me. If-if that's what you want – "

He tipped her head up until her eyes, dark with embarrassment, met his.

"But what do you want, Morag? What do you want so much that you'll beg for it? When will you take because you need to take more than you need the luxury of giving? That's what you have to pay for *my* pride!'

There was no answer to that. She had never gone down on her knees to anyone and she never would. Not even for the kisses of Pericles Holmes! But she felt cold when he took his hand away and colder still when he turned his back on her and left her alone with her own chaotic thoughts.

They left Athens Airport in bright sunshine with a a temperature of more than ninety degrees and came down three hours later into a wet, windy day in London that made for a rough landing and a quick dash from the aeroplane to the nearby terminal buildings. Rather to

Morag's surprise, her whole family assembled to meet her and, while she was waiting for Pericles to collect their suitcases and carry them through the Green Channel of the Customs, she caught sight of them waiting on the other side and she was struck anew by her stepsister's pale looks and the confident way she looked about her, sure that she was attracting every male eye in the place. Nor was her confidence misplaced. Morag watched, with what she told herself was amusement, as a good-looking young man brushed against Delia's shoulder, turned with a wide grin to apologise, and immediately stayed to make the most of the incident.

"So that is Delia," Pericles murmured in her ear. "What a very dishy young woman!" Stung, Morag wished she could deny it. "I told you she was," she answered. "I told you that you'd like her too!"

Pericles looked amused. "So you did. Do you think it's too soon for me to give her a brotherly kiss of greeting?"

Morag didn't bother to reply. It didn't matter what she did, she thought, Delia was bound to take over, and Pericles would follow her lead, and it would be just like David all over again. *Any* man had only to see Delia to want to kiss her.

She cast Pericles a swift, reproachful look and was not surprised to see he was smiling. It was an anticipatory smile, as if he already knew just how much he was going to enjoy dallying with Delia. Well, if she had anything to do with it, he would not be given the opportunity!

"I don't think it would be at all suitable! she snapped," her head held high. "Besides, you owe me something too! Or have you forgotten already?"

His smile grew deeper and she thought it had a rather triumphant air to it. "I haven't forgotten," he said. "You won't have any cause for complaint – while we're in England. Afterwards – "

"Afterwards we'll be back in Greece with the children,"

57

she attempted humour. "It won't matter then!"

"I expect your family will come out and stay with us from time to time. I certainly mean to do all I can to see that we stay on good terms with *all* of them!"

I'll bet! she thought. And all this after one glimpse of Delia! What was it going to be like when he had spent a whole week in her company?

Delia settled the whole question of the kiss by coming straight up to Pericles and offering him her face. "I ought to congratulate you," she said huskily, "but I know Morag too well to do that. I think I'll congratulate her instead! How did she manage to find an Adonis like you, even in the wilds of Greece?"

"I expect she'll tell you herself," Pericles answered smoothly. He turned away to shake Morag's father's hand and to be introduced to her stepmother. When he felt he had made himself sufficiently agreeable to them both, he put an arm about Morag's shoulders and smiled down at her.

Morag was so busy reminding herself that he didn't mean what his smile was telling her that she was quite unprepared for her stepsister's sudden exclamation.

"My dear Morag, where did you get that dreadful necklace? Let's have a look at it!" She pulled at the shells which Morag had put on under her jumper and laughed out loud. "It would be quite pretty if it weren't for those terrible green beads! Morag, you ought to know better than to wear such rubbish."

"I like them!" Morag declared.

Pericles grinned at her. He pulled the necklace out from under her jumper and rearranged it round her neck, making, she felt, the most of the moment and plainly enjoying her own shy attempts to prevent him.

"I gave them to her," he told the others. "She's under the protection of the goddess Nemesis when she wears them – "

"Yes, but I don't believe that!" Morag protested.

"Then why wear them now, darling?" he said.

"I thought they'd get crushed in my suitcase." It wasn't true. She hadn't thought about it at all. But it seemed as good a reason as any other. She would not admit, even to herself, that it was because he had given them to her. She had worn them constantly ever since, hiding them under her dress, or with a scarf round her neck. It was the *only* thing he had given her!

"Nemesis?" Delia said vaguely. "Seem to have heard about her. Doesn't she creep up behind people, dropping swords on their heads?"

Pericles frowned. "Not swords, no. I don't think you can have the right lady." He sounded short to the point of rudeness.

"No," Mr. Grant said soberly. He gave his stepdaughter an affectionate look mixed with admiration. "Delia's facts are always well chosen to suit herself. Nemesis sought out and punished evildoers."

"And compensated those who suffered," Morag put in, not looking at Delia. "I went to visit her temple in Greece."

Delia managed a very creditable smile. "What a good thing she has no jurisdiction in England!" she shot at Morag.

Mrs. Grant giggled. "Goodness, yes! But we mustn't bring up any painful memories for Morag today. She has obviously forgotten all about David – poor boy! We must try and do the same, Delia. After all, he was *her* fiancé!"

Morag coloured guiltily, seeking to evade Pericles' restraining arm while she thought of some devastating retort. But Pericles would not allow it. He gave Mrs. Grant a cool, considering look and then he smiled.

"Perhaps Morag had less to forget," he drawled. "Calf-love is painful at the time, especially when one's beloved is not particularly faithful, or particularly particular, come to that, but one grows out of such foolishness!"

Morag gave him a look of exasperation. "Calf-love?"

He raised an eyebrow, grinning. "Wasn't it?"

Her cheeks burned. "I suppose you know best," she managed to say.

He flicked her cheek with a gentle finger, but his attention had already wandered and she knew, without looking at him, that he was covertly studying her stepsister.

It was strange to be back in her father's house and to sleep in the room which had been hers all through her childhood. From the window she could see the stretch of road where that fateful evening the car had come weaving towards the gates, only to crash into the telegraph-pole on the far side of the road. Morag stood at the window for a long time, trying to recall what it was that she had felt then that had compelled her to take Delia's place at the wheel, after hurrying her stepsister up into the house and telling her to call the police. She must have been mad! How could she have thought that David mattered so much to her that his lightest interest had to be protected at such a cost?. She sighed, glad that it was getting dark and that it was time to change her dress. She had brooded for long enough. She had other things to think about now. Pericles, for example.

Coming home had had one unlooked-for advantage in that she was reunited with her wardrobe and no longer had to make do with what she had been able to carry in her knapsack. It took her all of ten minutes to decide which dress to wear. Her stepmother thought it was unlucky to wear green and so Morag had only one dress of that colour, and she chose it now, knowing that it brought out the green of her eyes and made her hair look darker and richer against the soft glow of the silk. Having made up her mind, it took her much less time to slip off the clothes she had been wearing, to put on a long petticoat, and to slide the green dress over her head, letting the wide skirt fall to her feet.

A knock at her door interrupted her efforts to pull up the zip behind her back.

60

"Come in," she called out. She heard the door open and went on quite crossly, "Do me up, will you? I think it's stuck!"

"Very pretty!" Pericles congratulated her.

She twisted round to face him. "I thought you were Delia!"

"Your father sent me up to fetch you. He wants to toast our health before dinner." His eyes looked her over with appreciation. "You'll have to turn round if you want me to fix your zip."

She turned her back, shivering as his fingers came in contact with her bare skin. "I wish Kimon and Peggy were here," she said. "They might have enjoyed all the fuss."

"Meaning that you're not?"

"Not much," she said.

"Then you don't want me to leave you here and to go back to Greece on my own?" She started undoing the few inches of zip he had managed to do up. "Oh, Perry, you wouldn't! Please don't tease me! I'll do *anything* –"

"Anything?"

Her hands clutched at and found his sleeve. "Y-yes," she stammered. "Only don't leave me here! You can't! You said you'd marry me!"

"You said you'd marry me, but I can't help wondering if you know what you're doing, Morag Grant. You're not marrying Kimon and Peggy!"

"I know that!"

A gleam of amusement lit his eyes. "I wonder. I think you're more intent on having some kind of revenge on your family. But it will be you who will have to live with it, *karthia mou*. I don't want you to rush into something you may regret."

She turned her back on him again, finding it easier not to look at him. "It isn't only that," she said. "I won't pretend that I'm not enjoying – well, you know how it is! You're so modest that you don't know that you're better than

61

good-looking and - very attractive! But I wouldn't make use of you like that!"

"Not even to get at Delia?"

Morag did not deign to reply as he finished zipping her up and turned her round to face him. "This is the last chance I shall give you to change your mind, Morag. I'll try not to rush you, but there can be no going back on your decision now."

She looked down, veiling her eyes with her long lashes. "I've said I want to marry you," she said quietly. "Isn't that enough?"

"I hope it will be – for you," he answered.

She looked up at him then, the colour creeping up her cheeks. "I don't know what you mean?"

He gave her a little shake. "I could beat you when you pretend to be obtuse!" he growled at her. "Don't count on my being patient with you for ever! One day I'll make you say it, all of it! You make a mistake if you think you can lead me by the nose for long! I am a man, and I won't play second fiddle to any chit of a girl. Is that clear enough for you?"

She nodded. "But you did promise that you'd pretend to be in love with me while we're here – Pericles, please – "

"Yes?"

But she couldn't go on. "You promised!" she said again.

His eyes narrowed and she was once more afraid of him. "I didn't promise to *pretend* anything. I promised to save your pride."

"But it's the same thing!"

"No, *yinéka mou*, it's not the same thing at all. Come on, we'd better go down to the others." He opened the door for her and stood back to let her pass. "By the way, did I tell you that I like your dress?"

She made a humble gesture with her hand and was surprised when he captured it in his own. To hide her pleasure, she rushed into speech. "You said you liked green. I put

62

it on for you!"

He bent and kissed her cheek. "Very pretty, *pedhi*, but it's the words I want, and it's the words I mean to have!"

It was strange to be married. Stranger still to find herself the equal of her stepmother and no longer the lesser loved daughter of the house. Morag enjoyed herself. She made the most of every moment of it from the time she walked down the aisle on her father's arm, for once the centre of his attention, right up to the last goodbye from the last of the guests.

True, it was a peculiarly solemn moment when she promised to love, honour, and obey him for the rest of her life, but the look in Pericles' eyes had started a blaze of hope that had stayed with her all day and even now had not quite died away.

"Happy, my dear?" her father asked her, easing himself out of his coat with a sigh of relief.

"Very happy!"

"You're a lucky girl. I don't mind telling you now that I was a bit worried about you and David. He didn't strike me as being your type – far more in Delia's line, if you know what I mean?"

"No, I don't," Morag said, frowning.

"Bit flashier in her tastes than you," her father rejoined. "He would have ended up with her – if he hadn't already. You're like your mother, and Delia is very like hers. I'm a lucky man to have known both. Don't misunderstand me, darling, my second marriage is a very happy one. One could not hope for the same generosity a second time such as your mother had. Is that what this Greek man has seen in you?"

"He's only half Greek."

Her father chuckled. "He looks Greek, and I daresay he makes love like a Greek. Did you tell him the truth about the David business, or did he guess?"

Morag gave him a quick glance. "I didn't think you knew!"

"I didn't know. I thought it likely, no more than that. I should have spoken up, I suppose. I didn't know what to do! I'm glad you've found someone to look after you. Too many people were ready to take advantage of you and you would have given them all everything you had. Pericles looks as though he knows how to keep you well in hand. I think you've chosen well there!"

Morag looked at him as though she had never really seen him before. "It was a lovely wedding, Daddy," she said. "Thank you for that."

"It was the least I could do. Ah, here's Delia. Did you enjoy the wedding too?" he asked his stepdaughter.

"Heavens, no! I thought it was rather pathetic, actually. Morag may think she's got Perry where she wants him, but it can't possibly last. I give her a year, and then he'll be bored with her as David was!"

"Delia!"

Delia smiled lazily at her stepfather. "Don't look so shocked! You know it's true! By the way, Morag, where are you going for your honeymoon? I suppose you are having one?"

Morag's eyes glittered dangerously. "I don't know," she admitted.

Delia laughed. "Well, hadn't you better find out?"

"Do you know?" Morag challenged her.

"Of course!"

Hurt to the quick, Morag ran from the room, running slap into Pericles in the hall. "How could you?" she demanded of him. "How could you tell *her* and not me?"

"Tell her what?"

"Where we're going!"

"But you know where we're going, Morag!"

"I don't!" she stormed at him. She lifted a hand as if to strike him, but he was before her, clipping both her wrists behind her back.

"We're going back to Greece, where else? Isn't that what you want?"

"Yes," she admitted uncertainly. "But why tell *her*?"

"Why let her know you mind?" he countered. He let her go with a suddenness that made her stagger. "How soon can you be ready to leave?"

"I haven't packed yet." She bit her lip. "I thought – "

He gave her a push towards the stairs, sighing. "Go and pack, Morag."

She met her stepmother coming down the stairs and stood aside for her to pass, hoping that she wouldn't notice how close she was to tears. It was a forlorn hope.

"Oh, Morag, I thought you would be gone! Crying already? I'm not surprised! It seems so strange for you to be the wife of a foreigner. I hope you manage to get used to their funny ways. Delia says it wouldn't do for her at all! Perry has been telling her some of the things that are expected of a wife in Greece. She says he only married you to look after the children anyway!"

Morag managed a light, amused laugh, helped on by the freezing anger that gripped her. She ran up the remaining stairs and threw her possessions into her suitcase, uncaring as to whether they creased or not. She shut the case with a bang and took a last look around the room. The necklace of shells lay on the bedside-table and she picked them up, longing to smash them as Peggy had smashed her necklace at Rhamous. Pericles had *promised*, and he hadn't even told her a simple thing like that they were going back to Greece. She put the shells round her neck, not knowing what else to do with them, and went downstairs again.

Pericles stood up the moment she appeared in the doorway. He took a step towards her, taking both her hands in his.

"Ready, darling? I have been trying to convince your father that we'll be pleased to see him any time in Athens.

65

You'll have to add your persuasions to mine!"

"But of course we'd love to have you," Morag heard herself say.

Her father chuckled. "When you've had time to get used to one another we might think about paying you a visit."

"Do, sir. Morag will like to see you, won't you, sweetheart?"

Morag felt hypnotised into agreeing with anything he said. She still felt cold with anger at his betrayal, but it didn't seem to matter very much. Nothing mattered, not even the acquisitive look in Delia's eyes that at another time would have filled her with despair.

"The car is waiting to take you to the airport," Mrs. Grant told them busily, her eyes snapping at the sight of Pericles holding Morag's hand. "I don't suppose you want us to come with you."

Pericles grinned at her. "Quite right. I haven't had an opportunity to kiss my bride yet, and where better than in a comfortable car?"

"Oh, but – " said Morag.

"She's shy," Delia said, sounding bored. "You'd think she'd never been kissed before!"

Pericles put his arms round Morag and hugged her tight, kissing her still pink cheek. "That's what I love about her," he said. "I'm Greek enough to want to come first with my wife." He kissed her again, very gently, but as if he meant it. "Do I come first?" he whispered in her ear.

She buried her face in his chest and clenched her fists, but she couldn't bring herself to say it. It was only to herself that she could acknowledge that with her he would always come first, last, and all the time, no matter what he did.

CHAPTER FIVE

"It sounds a funny sort of wedding to me," Kimon said.

"You look just the same as before,".Peggy added.

She felt just the same too, Morag reflected. The trip to England and the few days spent with her family were like the events of a dream. Pericles had hurried her into the car that had taken them to the airport, but he hadn't kissed her. All he had said was that she must be tired after such a long day and that he hoped she wouldn't find the flight back to Greece too much for her.

Morag had been aware of a dull feeling of disappointment which had lasted for the whole length of the journey. She had felt like a puppet, having her passport stamped and her luggage checked, and even when she had sat in the car beside Pericles for the short drive to his mother's villa.

Once they had arrived there, she had been sure that everything would change for the better, but it had not.

She had got out of the car, stiff-limbed and more than a little weary, but undeniably glad to be back in this lovely house, with its private pathway down to the sea. It had looked grey in the moonlight and friendly, just as she had remembered it.

"Aren't you glad to be home?" she had said to Pericles as he had bent to pick their luggage out of the boot.

"Is it home to you already?" he had smiled at her.

She had been a bit suprised herself, but there had been no doubt in her own mind that this was home, whereas her father's house had been no more than a memory of child-hood to her. She had nodded her head, feeling lost and a bit presumptuous for implying that Kyria Holmes' villa in some way belonged to her too.

"I expect my mother and the children are already in bed and asleep," he had said, catching up with her at the front door. "Which is where you ought to be. I'll put your things in your old room and you can stay there for tonight."

She had felt quite unable to argue with him about it, especially as she knew from experience how the slightest sound echoed up and down the hall, and the last thing she had wanted was to have Pericles' mother out on them. Besides, she had reasoned, feeling more and more leaden by the minute, it would only be for the one night, or what was left of it, and she could make the change into his room the following day. She had known, of course, that she would never find the courage to suggest such a thing herself, but she had been confident that he would insist on it, if for no better reason than for the look of the thing.

But he had done nothing of the sort. In fact he had done nothing at all. She might just as well not be married to him at all! She had hardly seen him in the last few days and, when she had seen him, she had found herself rendered almost completely tongue-tied, so nervous had she been of saying anything untoward. She was bound to admit that he had been more than patient with this sudden affliction that had taken her, but then perhaps he hadn't noticed that she had lost her tongue and that she started like a nervous rabbit whenever he looked at her! Oh, how she despised herself when she thought of it!

"I'm glad you went," Peggy assured her happily. "You wouldn't have brought back my stamp collection if you hadn't gone."

"It wasn't much fun while you were away, though," Kimon told her. "I much prefer it when you are here. Daddy says he does too."

Morag's heart lurched within her. When had he said that? she wondered.

"What do you want to do this afternoon?" she asked the children. "We could take the bus somewhere, if you like?"

"Athens," said Kimon with decision.

"It's too hot in Athens," Peggy argued. "I'd rather go swimming."

Kimon made a face at her. "You always want to go swimming!" He gave Morag a sudden smile that was very like his father's. "What do you want to do? You ought to choose sometimes too."

"You like swimming!" Peggy reminded her quickly, anxious that she was not going to get her own way after all.

"Yes, I do. But we went swimming this morning. I'd like to go to Athens too. I want to do some shopping –"

Both children groaned at that. "I hate shopping!" Kimon muttered. His face brightened, though, as a new idea struck him. "Yes, you go shopping, and we can go to the museum and see all the different coins there. I want to compare my Spartan coin with the ones they have there. We'd be quite all right on our own in the museum, truly we would! And we could all have an ice-cream outside afterwards."

"Yes," said Peggy. "I like to see the man there carrying a mountain of things on his tray. I don't know how he remembers who wants what. May we do that, Morag?"

Glad to have found a compromise so easily, Morag said they would go immediately after lunch. Kyria Holmes, when told of the plan, thought at first she would like to go with them, but in the end she decided against it.

"Since you talked me into painting again," she said to her daughter-in-law with a wry smile, "I have done little else. You must tell me if you think any of my canvases are good enough to show to Pericles."

"I don't know if I'd know," Morag told her. "I'd love to see them, though. Are they all landscapes?"

"No, not at all." The older woman's eyes glinted in the sunlight. "I've been meaning to ask you to call me Dora," she said. "I don't think I should care for Mama – it's bad

69

enough that Perry calls me that! – and we can't go on being formal for ever."

Morag's face was filled with surprised pleasure. "Thank you," she murmured.

Dora gave her an amused look. "I'm glad you like living here," she went on coolly. "Pericles is afraid that you may be lonely as he had so much business to get through, but you seem to fill your days pretty well. I find it hard to believe as he does that you want your family to visit you quite yet! But you have only to ask – you know there is plenty of room!"

Morag answered quickly, "I don't think they'd want to come quite yet!"

"No? Your stepsister longs to come to Greece, I'm told. Pericles says she's a raving beauty. Perhaps I should paint her some time."

Morag swallowed down the comment that beauty is as beauty does with difficulty. She thought Dora might have some difficulty in understanding the allusion, but she couldn't possibly mistake the tone.

"If Pericles wants to ask her," she began, "I should – should have no objection."

Dora shrugged, unmoved by these wifely sentiments. "You'd better tell him that! But I should remember my dear, that Pericles is a man like any other, and the Greeks have always found it very hard to resist physical beauty – especially when there is nothing else to distract them!"

Morag shrugged her shoulders. "That's not my fault!"

"No?" Morag, who had grown daily more at ease with Pericles' mother, had forgotten how imperious she could be. "It would only take a word from you –"

"*No*! He arranged things this way. I'm not going to *ask* him for anything!"

Dora shrugged again. "Have you ever thought that it's more generous sometimes to take than to give? Why don't you have it out with him once and for all? At least he'd know what you wanted from him, and not just what you are willing to give, no matter how willingly!"

Morag shrank away from her impatience. "I couldn't," she said in a small voice.

"But how is he to know you're in love with him if you don't tell him?" her mother-in-law demanded unanswerably.

"You don't think he's guessed?" Morag asked faintly.

"Oh, don't ask me! I'm only his mother! You'd better get on to Athens and do your shopping before I start giving you some very bad advice which you won't take. I doted on my own husband, not that he cared whether I did or not as long as I was there to fulfil his needs. But Pericles is different. I'd say it was his English blood, but what else was his father? Susan's indifference worried him very much, though she could hardly have married young Takis, no matter how much in love with him she fancied herself to be. Love grows after marriage, if you let it, but Pericles won't see that. I can't think why he married you!"

Morag's eyes filled with tears. "Why don't you ask him?"

"My dear child, I keep telling you that Pericles is a full-grown man! I have no right to ask him any such thing. A man's life is his own. It's quite different for a woman. It's her nature to respond and not to initiate, so she can be taught to love and to live her life subordinate to her husband's. That is the Greek way!"

"Perry is only half Greek!"

Dora laughed. "Maybe, but he's man enough for you, Morag Holmes, as you'll find out one of these days!"

It wasn't a very auspicious start to the afternoon and, by the time she had collected the children, they had missed the bus and had to wait for the next one in the burning heat of the afternoon, a prospect that didn't please any of them. Morag and Peggy sat on a low wall by the side of the road, but Kimon was made of sterner stuff and spent the time spotting the different makes of cars that flashed past him.

"Look, there's Takis!" he shouted after a few minutes. "He'll take us to Athens. Make him stop, Morag! He won't be able to see me!"

Morag stood up and waved her scarf half-heartedly. She rather hoped that Takis would go by without stopping, but with a screech from his brakes he drew in beside them, grinning broadly.

"How can I serve you, Morag? Do you wish me to carry you away from all your troubles?"

"What troubles?" Peggy asked him, not at all pleased that he should have spoken only to Morag thus, ignoring Kimon and herself.

"What troubles? You and Kimon are the biggest troubles. Her other ones she prefers to keep to herself! Well, Morag, where do you want to go?"

"We want to go to Athens, but we missed the bus and the next one doesn't come for another twenty minutes."

"Then of course I shall take you! You see how I feel about you that your lightest desire is my immediate command. You shall sit beside me and we shall forget all about the children in the back and have a nice time. Is that what you'd like?"

"Not much," she answered frankly. "I wouldn't ask you to take us at all if it weren't so hot!"

"You are unkind!" Takis complained.

"Very!" she agreed.

The young Greek exploded into laughter. "Unkind, but funny! Climb in, children. One is not allowed to stop here and a policeman may come at any moment. Have you enough room, Morag? You can come closer. *I* do not mind!"

Morag sat as far away from him as possible, trying not to notice the handle that was sticking into her ribs, or his straying hand that somehow found her knee every time he changed gear.

"We're going to the Museum," Peggy told him. "I'd rather have gone swimming, but we're going to meet

72

Morag for an ice-cream outside afterwards."

"Oh? And where do you spend your afternoon, Morag?" Takis asked.

"I've got some shopping to do," she said reluctantly.

He flashed her a smile. "What do you buy? A new dress? I shall come with you and help you choose! I have a very good eye for buying dresses."

"I'd rather you didn't."

"No woman should go shopping by herself," he declared. "They need someone to tell them that look beautiful in one dress, or more desirable in another. You will see, I am very good at escorting women and I always know exactly the right thing to say! Besides, I can translate all your wishes to the assistants and make sure you get what you want."

Morag sighed. She decided complete honesty was the only way to deal with him and she scurried round her mind for the right words in which to tell him that she didn't want his company. "Takis, please leave me alone. P–Pericles wouldn't like it, and I don't like it either!"

His eyebrows rose in complete disbelief. "P–Pericles," he mimicked her. "Do you mind about him?"

"Of course I do!"

"He doesn't seem to return the compliment! If you were my bride, you would not be waiting for a bus under the hot sun! He deserves that you should look elsewhere for a little fun. Why doesn't he buy you a car?"

Morag hesitated. Then, "I don't drive," she confessed.

"Pericles could teach you!"

Morag felt more uncomforable and hot than ever. "I can drive, only I don't, so it's my own choice to wait around for buses. Pericles –"

"Could drive you himself!"

"Why should he? He has better things to do with his time!"

"But I haven't? From now on I am your chauffeur.

You have only to ask and I shall be there to drive you!"

"No, Takis. If I wanted anyone to drive me, I'd ask Pericles! It was only this afternoon when we missed the bus and Kimon saw you that we needed a lift. Usually we can manage very well by ourselves!"

"No thanks to Pericles!"

Morag glared at him. "I won't have you sneering at him!" she retorted. "He's very kind to me, and I love him very much!"

Takis lost some of his bounce and began to apologise. "I hadn't realised that you felt like that about him," he protested. "I thought it was a suitable arrangement for you both. Though I still feel he could look after you better!" His smile came back, and he patted her knee. "You defend him just like a Greek wife!" he teased her. "Are you as meek as a Greek wife should be to Pericles?"

Morag looked determinedly out of the window. She saw with relief that they were almost in Athens. "I try to be," she said.

Takis chuckled. "It would be interesting to find out if he defends you with the same fervour. He was never in the least bit strict with Susan." He drove in silence all the rest of the way into the centre of Athens, only asking her where she wanted to be put down. "There's a place to park just by the temple of Olympian Zeus. Will that be too far for you to walk?"

Morag had no idea, but she was in no mood to argue with him. "Of course not," she said with a confidence she was far from feeling.

"But it is!" Kimon insisted, breaking abruptly into the argument he had been having with his sister ever since they had set foot into the car. "Can't you take us right to the museum, Takis? Or to Omonia Square?"

"If you like," the Greek agreed easily. He pointed out the Royal Guard outside the Parliamentary buildings, dressed in the short white kilts, white stockings, and long shoes with their pouffs on the toes.

"Along here are the shops," Peggy told Morag. "Grandma buys her clothes here. They're very good shops, but there aren't any department stores like in London – at lesst, I don't think there are. You won't get lost, will you?"

"No, of course I won't get lost!" Morag protested. "I'll come and see you into the museum first."

Takis stopped the car and leaned across her to open the door. "You're not still cross with me, are you, Morag?" he asked her, smiling straight into her eyes. "Tell me you are not! Please let me come back to the cafe outside the museum in an hour's time and buy you all an ice-cream? Then I shall know that you've forgiven me!"

Morag hesitated and knew, even while she did so, that it was a mistake. "I think it would be better if you didn't," she began, but he had already noted her lack of decision.

"You couldn't be so cruel as to deny me!" he pleaded. "The children will like to have me there!" He rubbed his hand through Kimon's hair. "Don't I buy you the best ice-creams?" he asked him.

"I suppose so," Kimon confirmed. He ducked away from his cousin. "But Daddy doesn't like us to eat too much between meals," he added somewhat primly.

"Then I shall come and sit at the next-door table and hope you take pity on me!" Takis declared. He watched them climb out of the car, his eyes dancing with amusement. "See you then!" he laughed and, with a wave of his hand, he was gone.

Morag frowned after him, but there was nothing to be done and so with a slight shrug of her shoulders she put him to the back of her mind and walked with the children through the formal gardens that led to the National Museum.

"Are you sure you'll be all right?" she fussed as she bought their tickets and gave them each some money to buy postcards or anything else they wanted.

"Of course we shall be!" Peggy insisted.

Kimon nodded. "We know what we want to see, you see," he pointed out. "I want to look at any coins I can find and Peggy wants to make a drawing of the little Jockey now that they've found the horse and mounted him on it. He does look rather super – *much* younger than we are!"

Morag, who had seen the statue when she had visited the museum before she had met any of the Holmes, was surprised. "I didn't know you liked to draw," she said to Peggy.

"Well, Grandma didn't like me to talk about it," the small girl explained, "but since she's started painting again, she doesn't mind my wasting my time drawing things half so much. She looked at some I'd done the other day and told me quite a lot of useful things to help me get the perspective right. She wasn't cross at all!"

"Wasn't she?" Morag smiled with real pleasure. "She must think you're good if she took the trouble to look at your work. She hasn't much time for the second-rate."

"No," Peggy agreed with all the assurance of one who knew that there was no danger of her every being considered that. "But I'm not as good as she is. She's done a *beautiful* painting of you!"

"Of me?"

"Yes," said Kimon. "She showed it to us while you were getting married in England. It looks quite like you, only I haven't seen you looking dreamy like she has. She said you looked like that when you thought about Daddy."

Morag was completely disconcerted. She longed to question them longer, but their impatience to be gone was so obvious that she hadn't the heart to keep them. "I'll be back in one hour exactly," she told them.

"Yes, all right. Don't fuss, Morag!"

Conscious that she was doing exactly that, Morag went out of the building again, reminding herself that, unlike herself, they both spoke excellent Greek and could always ask someone if they couldn't find their way back to the main doors. It would be far more difficult for her to manage her shopping than it would be for them to spend an hour on their own in the museum.

She walked down one of the main streets that went between Omonia and Syntagma Squares, shamelessly window-shopping. She thought she was justified in buying herself a new dress. She had not discussed money with Pericles, and she had no idea whether he eventually intended to make her some kind of an allowance, or whether she would have to ask him whenever she was in need. But this money was her own. She had brought it with her to finance her trip through Greece and she had only spent very little of it. It cost her nothing to live at Dora's villa beyond her few personal needs. Then the idea had come to her that she would buy herself a new dress. It had to be no ordinary dress, but something very special, something that would flatter her into a kind of beauty. She had not forgotten how Pericles had looked at her that evening that she had worn her green dress and she wanted badly for him to look at her like that again. Not even Delia's best efforts to divert his attention to herself had quite succeeded that evening. If, Morag thought, she could find herself a truly splendid dress, perhaps he would look at her again in the same way, he might even want to kiss her again, kiss her as he had not kissed her ever since their wedding.

The first shop she entered had nothing that caught her eye, but in the second shop was a dress made of cloth of gold and cut in a style that she knew immediately would suit her. She pointed silently at it when the assistant came to serve her and for a second they both gazed at the dress in silence.

"It's beautiful!" Morag breathed.

The assistant nodded sympathetically. "It is also expensive," she murmured in very creditable English. "Do you want to try it?"

Morag nodded. She didn't care how expensive it was, she had to have it. If *that* didn't have the desired effect on

Pericles, she would write herself off as a total failure and that didn't even bear thinking about.

"How much is it?" she asked timidly as the assistant gathered up the full skirt and threw it over her head. She held her breath and watched the gold cloth ripple down to her ankles. It shimmered, trembling just as she had trembled when Pericles had touched her. She didn't care how much it cost, she had to have it!

Even so the price came as a jolt to her. "Are you sure?" she exclaimed, unable to take her eyes off her gleaming reflection in the glass.

"Yes, *kyria*, I am very sure."

Morag sighed. If she paid such a sum on a single dress, she would have nothing left of her own. It would serve her right, for it would be sheer extravagance to spend her all on a single dress, and a dress that she was not likely to wear often at that.

"I'll take it!"

She felt quite dazed with her own bravado. She had to keep looking at the dress to reassure herself all over again as she countersigned the traveller's cheques she had brought with her. The assistant glanced at her wedding-ring with a little smile.

"I hope he knows! Or is it to surprise him?"

"It's a surprise," Morag admitted. "It's my own money, so he can't be very angry –" She broke off as a decidedly male hand covered one of hers and Takis squinted at the bill beside the empty plastic cover to her traveller's cheques.

"Phew!" he whistled.

The Greek girl picked the gold dress off the rail and held it up for him to see. "Your wife has chosen well. She looked magnificent –"

"She always looks lovely!" Takis cut her off.

Only Morag seemed to have noticed the Greek girl's mistake. "He isn't –"

78

Takis silenced her with a quick kiss on the side of her mouth. "My wife thinks I'm marvellous! You see, I never question how much she spends on clothes!"

"A nice husband to have!" the Greek girl said admiringly. "Shall I wrap the dress, *kyria*, or do you want us to send it?"

"I'll–I'll take it with me," Morag stammered, her mouth dry.

Takis flashed his bright smile. "I'll carry it for her, so put a decent handle on it. I don't like it when the string cuts into my fingers."

The girl gave him a look of pure adulation and hurried away to fold and wrap the dress.

"I wish you hadn't come, Takis," said Morag. "I did ask you not to."

"And who would have carried your packages then?"

"And another thing," Morag went on, warming to her theme, "how dare you give the impression that you're my husband?"

He put a finger across her lips to silence her. "Better that than that she should jump to a different conclusion, my sweet innocent. You wouldn't like it if she thought I was *not* your husband, would you?"

She glared at him. "I'll carry my own package!" she snapped, almost snatching it out of the assistant's hands. "I can keep my eye on it then!"

Takis shrugged and winked at the Greek girl. "Tell me when you are tired and then I will carry it," he smiled.

Morag could hardly refuse his company back to the museum. It would have been silly to have walked ahead because she knew he would only follow on behind making her feel a fool.

As if he had read her thoughts, Takis put a hand on her shoulder and smiled his little boy smile. "You won't make me sit at a separate table for my ice-cream, will you, Morag? I'm doing my best to please you!"

She gasped with suppressed fury. "Your best! Perhaps you should try your worst for a change!"

He grinned. "If you like. My worst would be to forget this foolish marriage of yours and kiss you a little myself. You're a pretty little thing, Morag *pedhi*, especially when you try to look cool and calm, and your eyes flash fire and promise –"

"They promise you nothing! Takis, if you go on like this, I shall tell Pericles – and Dora!"

"Dora would blame you. No man is ever to blame for flirting with a pretty girl in her opinion. I think you won't say anything to Thia Dora. And you are too afraid of Pericles to mention any escapade to him. No, no, you value his opinion of you too highly to risk his taking you to task for playing games with me!"

Morag hurried her footsteps, her indignation reverberating along the pavement. "I'll never speak to you again!" she told him furiously. "Why won't you go away?" But he only laughed and took her new dress from her, tucking it under his arm as he put a hand on her elbow to guide her across the busy street.

If Morag would have rather that he was anywhere else, the children were more than pleased to him, however. They were already seated at one of the tables that had been arranged under the trees in the forecourt of the museum.

"We didn't order until you came," Kimon mentioned quickly. "We thought Takis might be with you."

"So I can pay, huh?" his cousin teased him. "Well, here I am! What are you all going to have?"

"Ice-cream," they demanded unanimously.

Takis looked at Morag, his eyes bright – too bright. "And you?"

She would have liked to have refused to have anything, but she thought that that would be making too much of a silly incident. Besides, it was terribly hot and the cooling breeze that always seemed to be present beside the sea was absent from the stifling Athens streets. She looked down her nose, sitting very straight in her chair. "I'll have a pressed lemon," she said.

Takis laughed. "I'll tell him to bring you plenty of sugar!" he teased her.

Morag averted her face. She rescued the box holding her dress from beside his chair where he had put it and hugged it to her. He had spoilt her whole afternoon, but at least she had her dress!

It was a long time before their order came. The waiter, when he did come, was carrying a huge tray, laden several layers deep with drinks, ice-creams, cakes and large, cool glasses of water that were served automatically with every order. Diverted for a moment from her anger with Takis, Morag watched the man making his way towards them and thought how well the Athenians laid out their cafés, making the best of every site, temporary or otherwise. Then, with a start of dismay, she realised that the waiter was not the only one who was coming towards them, for behind him came Pericles, a Pericles looking so grim that she clutched her package closer still for comfort.

"Daddy!" Peggy exclaimed. "Daddy, what are you doing here?"

Pericles' eyes rested on Morag's face. "I came to take you home. Are you ready to go?"

She nodded helplessly, as tongue-tied as she always was in his presence nowadays.

"But you haven't had your pressed lemon," Kimon reminded her, his voice tinged with indignation. "Nor have we had our ice-creams!" he added.

Pericles put his hand on Morag's feet, the steely pressure of his fingers drawing her to her feet. "Then you two can come home with Takis," he ordered them. "Morag will come with me – now!"

Morag clutched her package and followed him to where he had left his car in silence. She wished that he would look a little less grim, or that she could think of something bright to say that would relieve the atmosphere between them.

"I thought I told you not to dally with Takis, or to be alone with him?" Pericles said smoothly in a voice that brought a wave of panic to the pit of her stomach.

"The children –" she began.

"The children! Were the children there when you went shopping together?"

In silence she shook her head. "I didn't ask him to come, Perry. He followed me to the shop."

He gave her a long, level look. "All right, Morag," he said at last. "But I shan't tell you a third time. Stay away from Takis, or I shall make it my business to see that you do! Now get in and I'll drive you home."

She did so, the tears stinging her eyes. He got in beside her and started the engine, but he didn't drive off immediately.

"Tears, Morag? Then see that you don't give me cause to get really angry with you because, by God, you'll be sorry if you do!"

Morag gave him a frightened look and thought he looked grimmer than ever. She had not the slightest difficulty in believing him. She was sorry now, though she didn't see how she could have got rid of Takis under the circumstances and, if she had felt braver, she would have said so. Pericles lifted an eyebrow and smiled suddenly.

"You could have refused to get into his car in the first place," he told her. "That was where you made your mistake."

And looking back over the afternoon, Morag could only agree with him.

CHAPTER SIX

"HAVE I any money?"

The question as it came out sounded bald and ungracious, and she immediately wished it unsaid, as happened so often with her nowadays.

Pericles glanced at the parcel she was still hugging to her. "I hadn't thought about it," he admitted. "I'm sorry, Morag. I should have done so. What have you been living on all this time?"

"I haven't needed much. I don't need much now. I only meant that it's nice to have a little, to give the children ice-creams occasionally, and things like that."

He gave her a wry look. "Is that an explanation of why you encouraged Takis to tag along? To pay for the children's ice-creams?"

She coloured. "No, of course not. I was only trying to explain why I needed money."

"My dear girl, if you buy all your clothes at that particular boutique you'll need more than a few drachmae to keep you going!" She found his amusement very hard to bear, but it was worse still when he added, "Did Takis suggest you went there too?"

"No."

He cast her a quick, curious glance. "I thought you brought all your clothes back from England with you?" he enquired.

"Yes, I did," she admitted. She knew he was going to ask her why she found it necessary to buy anything more and she had no answer ready for him. How could she confess that she had deliberately gone out to buy a dress that would transform her into the woman of his dreams, and not just the girl whom he had married as a convenience to look after his children! "But one doesn't want to wear old clothes for ever. I'm sure your mother must be sick of the sight of me in jeans. She's very – elegant herself, isn't she?"

"I don't think she minds your jeans," he said, still looking amused. "Is this new dress to take their place?"

"Not exactly," she said. Was it likely that she'd wear an evening dress of cloth of gold in the middle of the afternoon? It made it all the more difficult to explain why she had bought it at all!

"Did you buy the dress for Takis?"

"Of course not!"

"I don't see that there's any of course about it," he returned with renewed anger. "He has a way with women – as I know to my cost!"

Morag felt an impatience with the dead Susan that made her long to tell Pericles once and for all how stupid she thought his wife had been. But there are limits as to what one can fittingly say about the dead, and she bit back the words, her mind working furiously as to how else she could convince him that Takis meant nothing to *her*, whatever emotion he had stirred in Susan's breast.

"I'm not surprised Takis is so spoilt," she said in an amused, cool voice that pleased her well. "You all go on about him as if he were something fantastically special. No wonder he believes it himself!"

Pericles' mouth tightened. "You have to admit he is handsome –"

"Do you think so?" Morag said in the same light tones.

"Don't you?"

Morag achieved a yawn. "In a way. Flashy good looks like his have never appealed to me much. I prefer –" She broke off. If she told him what she preferred, he would be bound to recognise himself in the picture she drew. "I prefer someone less obvious – stronger, if you know what I mean, who doesn't have to play-act all the time."

84

"Does he play-act?" He sounded as thought it were a new thought to him and one that he rather liked.

"All the time. He's the biggest ham I've ever met!"

"Well, well," he murmured. "And what makes you think you prefer the iron hand in the velvet glove? I haven't noticed you giving way to anyone or anything, except when one of those sudden impulses of yours takes you by storm."

"I may have been impulsive over David, but I've got over that." She glanced at him covertly through her eye-lashes. "I wish I'd never told you that Takis is like him! You've been quite horrid and suspicious ever since! And anyway, David had more substance that Takis, even if he wasn't all that I'd thought him. You make me sound a perfect idiot!"

"Didn't you also marry me on impulse?" he said.

She refused to answer. Was that what he believed of her? It seemed to her only too likely, and it was a depressing thought to her that she could see no way of denying the charge without telling him why she had married him, and she wasn't ready to do that, even if she could have found the words to do so.

"Well?" he prompted her.

Morag bit her lip in displeasure, frowning out of the window. "You don't understand!" she said. "You don't understand me, and I don't think you understood Susan either!" She put a hand quickly up to her mouth. "I didn't mean –"

His hands tightened on the steering-wheel and he slowed the car down to a crawl. "What did you mean?" he asked in the inflexible dangerous tones that she knew so well.

"Only that I'm not as silly as you think!"

He stopped the car altogether. "Aren't you, my dear?"

She shook her head, swallowing hard. "I'm not a child!" she almost shouted. "You go on as if I do nothing but jump from one scrape into another!"

She knew he was looking at her and that she wouldn't be

able to read his expression even if she could bring herself to look back at him. She began picking at her fingers instead, unconsciously betraying the nervousness that she most wanted to hide from him.

"If you do," he said, "this is one scrape you won't get out of in a hurry! You had your chance to change your mind. It's too late for you to do so now!" He went on watching her, then he put a hand over hers, forcing her to be still. "Why don't you think I understood Susan?"

"I don't know," she admitted.

"You must have some reason for saying such a thing!"

She hesitated. Then, "I don't believe she preferred Takis," she said at last in a small voice. "Not unless you made her think she did."

"Oh?" his voice was wintry in the extreme. She made a restless movement with her hands, but he had no intention of releasing his hold on them.

"She couldn't have done!"

His eyebrows rose at that. "Why not?"

"Because she married you!"

One corner of his mouth turned down. "She didn't have much choice. Her family saw to that, aided and abetted by mine. Love and romance didn't come into the matter. It's not unusual in Greece, you know."

Morag bent her head. "I can't explain," she muttered. "I knew you wouldn't understand!"

"On the contrary, I think I do understand. I find it a very interesting point of view!"

She shrugged her shoulders. "Yes, well, aren't we going home? Takis and the children will be there before us if we don't hurry."

"Does that matter?" he drawled.

"Of course!" she said. "It's my job to look after them!"

She saw him smile. "As my wife, your job is whatever I say it is. The children will be all right without you for a few minutes. Now, let's talk about you. How much money do

86

you think you'll need each month?"

She was so relieved that Pericles wanted to talk about money and nothing more personal that she looked up with a quick intake of breath. Her eyes met his and dropped into his hand which was still covering hers. "It's very hot. Takis had ordered a pressed lemon for me, but you took me away before I could drink it. You might at least have waited until I'd had a sip from it!"

"Is that a hint that I should find a café and buy you a drink?"

She nodded, feeling more at ease. "If we don't have to worry about the children. And if you can spare the time?" She turned on him, suddenly aware that it was the middle of the afternoon and that he ought to be working. "Why are you here anyway?"

His expression was indulgent. "Would you rather I went away?"

"No, but shouldn't you be working?"

He glanced at his watch. "I think I can spare you a few minutes. Besides, I could do with a drink too."

He chose a café overlooking the sea. He pulled out a chair for her and sat down himself opposite her, watching her closely. When the waiter came for their order, he gave it in Greek without consulting her. Morag presumed that he had ordered another pressed lemon for her, but when it came there was a cottage type bowl of yoghurt, rich and creamy, which he pushed over to her side of the table. "It's very good for the complexion," he told her.

She found it very refreshing. It was cold and sour, but not too sour. It was much richer than the yoghurt she had known in England, but she thought perhaps it was because this was obviously home-made and had no other flavour, or real fruits added. It disappeared quickly and she had practically finished it before she became aware that Pericles was still watching her with the same close attention.

"Aren't you going to have any?" she asked him.

"I was going to have half yours. Didn't you have any lunch?"

"Oh," she said. "I'm sorry. You should have told me before." She smiled. "You're too late now, it's all gone!"

"I'll make do with my lager." He paused. "Why did you buy the dress, Morag?"

She licked her spoon thoughtfully, and then took a sip of the ice-cold water which had actually come with Pericles' beer but which she didn't think he was going to drink himself. "No particular reason," she said.

"Shall I tell you what I think?" He picked up the parcel that held her dress. "I think you plan to dazzle someone –"

She retained her composure with an effort. "I plan to dazzle all of you!" she said quickly. "No one in particular!"

Pericles looked into the parcel, fingering the cloth of gold. "Dazzle is the word!"

"Yes." Her enthusiasm for the dress rekindled. "Don't you think it's beautiful? It cost every penny I had, but I can't regret it! I won't regret it."

He pushed the parcel across the table to her. "When are you going to wear it?"

"I don't know. I thought perhaps Dora would give a party for us, after the summer when most people start coming back to Athens." She looked up at him again. "Not a big party – just friends and relations?"

"You mean my friends and relations?"

"Mine are all still in England," she reminded him, yet instinctively thinking of Delia. "Besides, they came to our wedding. I thought now that we're married, you'd want to introduce me to your friends. I didn't mean to take too much for granted."

"No, you don't ask much, do you? Why not, Morag? If you want a party, why don't you insist on one?"

She pulled her dress towards her, deliberately avoiding his eyes. "You might not like it."

"And that matters?"

88

She nodded, taking another sip from his glass of water. "I wish you wouldn't look at me like that."

A smile creased his face. "Why not?"

"I never know what you're thinking."

"Just as well," he commented.

She gave him a quick look. "I don't see why," she began. "It would be much easier if I knew what you wanted. I always seem to guess wrong!"

He laughed. "All right," he said, "I'll tell you exactly what I was thinking. I was wondering what you'd do if I drove you up into the hills and made love to you. Would you like that, *karthia mou*?"

She pressed the dress to her bosom. "You – you wouldn't!"

Pericles rose to his feet with a nonchalant ease that she could only envy. "You are my wife!" he reminded her. He picked up the bill from the table and put down a few coins to pay it. "Are you coming, Morag?"

"Pericles, you haven't said if I may have some money?"

A gust of laughter broke from him. "There is a difficulty," he told her. "If I open a bank account for you, you'd have to write out your cheques in Greek. Will you settle for a joint account?"

"Oh, but I only want a few pounds a month!"

"Okay, I'll give you cash and you can let me know if you need any more." He took the parcel out of her arms. "I'll throw in this for good measure. How's that?"

She gave him a cautious smile. "It was terribly expensive."

"I knew that as soon as I saw the label!" he said. He lowered his voice to an intimate murmur. "If I pay for it, don't you think you might tell me why you bought it?"

Morag preceded him out of the café, glad of the opportunity to turn her back on him and thus avoid the mocking brilliance of his glance. "It was an impulse," she lied.

He shook his head at her. "You're a bad fibber, Morag. One day I'll have the truth from you, the whole truth!"

She gave him a quick look. "But –"

"I know," he said. "I said I wouldn't rush you! But don't take too long, *pedhi*, in finding the words, or I may decide to do without them before we come to terms. I don't think you'll hold out against me for long!" He put her into the car and handed her the parcel. "You shall have your party. I'll speak to my mother about it. You're right about that too. I should introduce my wife to my friends." He bent his head and kissed her on the cheek. "It'll give you a chance to get used to the idea too," he added meaningly. "No Greek waits for long on the convenience of a woman – and remember, I am half Greek!"

As if she were likely to forget it! It was part of his attraction for her, that she also knew! She cursed her own cowardice that had stopped her taking up his offer to drive her up into the hills for the afternoon. How wonderful it would have been! If she shut her eyes she could almost smell the thyme that scented the barren slopes behind the coast, and the pine-trees if one happened on a clump of them, and even the inevitable goats, their bells sounding as they scampered over the rocky outcrops that littered the brown-grey background of the Apollon Coast.

The children were home before them. "Where have you been?" they demanded of their father, suspicious that they had been left out of some treat.

"I wanted Morag to myself for a while," he answered. "We don't get enough time to ourselves."

Peggy smiled up at him in a peculiarly feminine way. "We've hardly seen you at all either, Daddy. And I particularly want to talk to you about something." She took his hand in hers. "Can I talk to you now?"

Kimon watched his sister and father disappear down the path towards the sea with a slight frown. "Did you get into trouble?" he asked Morag.

"Whatever for?"

"Oh, I don't know. I just thought you might have bought it from Daddy. He used to hate it when Mummy went out with Takis – he doesn't like him, you know. They used to row like anything about it, but Mummy wouldn't pay any attention. She said we weren't in Greece often enough for it to matter."

Morag swallowed, a little shocked that Kimon should have been allowed to see so much of his parents' differences.

"No, I don't think he does like Takis," she agreed out loud. "But I explained about his giving us a lift into Athens –"

Kimon gave her a cheeky look. "Are you scared of Daddy? You looked it when he took you away!"

"Certainly not!"

"Not even a little bit? Did you tell him that Takis helped you choose your new dress? I'll bet you didn't!"

"Then you bet wrong! He already knew that Takis had followed me to the shop." She flushed a little and smiled too. "Your father likes my dress, if you want to know. He's going to give it to me for a present!"

"Phew!" said Kimon with dawning respect. "You must have spun him a yarn! Takis said he'd more likely beat you!"

Morag made a little gesture of distaste. "He shouldn't talk to you like that. I think Pericles is right. I don't like him very much either."

"No, you wouldn't," Kimon agreed calmly. "Most people like him, though, especially girls, because he never seems to do any work and he has lots of money. That's why Mummy liked him. She said he was good fun, but I think he's a creep! Only he does buy us a lot of ice-cream too!"

Morag merely looked at him and Kimon made a face at her. "Peggy likes him," he went on hastily, "because he tells her she's pretty, and she likes that."

Not for the first time, Morag thought how much shrewder Kimon was than his sister. She was glad to have won the liking and affection of them both, but it was Kimon's respect she wanted because she felt it was worth more than

Peggy's. Peggy was too easy to bribe with pretty words and pretty things.

She looked down at the sea, to where she could see Pericles and Peggy standing below her, and she tried not to mind that he had only chosen her so that she could look after his children.

"So we are to have a party," Dora said. "Pericles says that it's your idea that we should introduce you to our friends." Her eyes lit with mocking laughter. "I hope you know what you're about! Pericles is not a party man by nature!"

"It won't do him any harm for once," Morag answered calmly.

"No, but I'm surprised he agreed to it all the same. He didn't give in to Susan so easily! Why should he indulge you?"

Morag, determined not to mind whatever her mother-in-law should say, merely smiled. "He wants to see me in my new dress," she explained. "He gave it to me," she added.

"So I heard," Dora said dryly.

Morag wondered what else she had heard and who could have told her. Takis? She wouldn't put it past him, for if he didn't get his own way, he liked to make trouble, rather as Peggy did sometimes, only Peggy did it far less now she was happier in herself, and Peggy was only ten years old.

"Why don't you show some of your paintings at the party?" she said to give her mother-in-law's thoughts another direction.

"Oh, I couldn't!" Dora said immediately.

"Why not?" Morag insisted. "I want to see them, and so does everyone else. I'm going to suggest it to Pericles, because I want Peggy to show some of hers too, but only if you think she's any good. She thrives on praise!"

Dora was not pleased. "How should I know if her stuff is any good? I don't know about my own any longer. I've got used to the idea that women have better things to do with their time than paint –"

"I think you know," Megan said simply.

"And what do you know about it?"

Morag bit her lip. "Not very much. But Perry does! That's why I'm hoping he'll persuade you. It would be so good for Peggy to be taken seriously by people outside her immediate family –"

"I suppose you think it would be good for me too!" Dora said with increasing irritation. "Well, you'll have to do better than that to persuade me!"

Morag managed a smile. "I have another reason," she admitted, "but I don't think you'll like it very much!"

Dora's look was one of enquiry. "You're a surprising person, Morag. Would you go on with this if Pericles didn't like the idea?"

Morag wished that she could say she would. "No," she said.

"I thought not," Dora congratulated herself. "Then I shall have a word with Pericles too. I think he's more likely to listen to me, don't you?"

Morag did, but she was not going to admit it. "Dora, please do this for me!"

Dora made a great play of rearranging her hair. "Are you asking for yourself?" She pulled her hair forward with a grimace. "Well, girl, what is this other reason I won't like?"

Morag came forward and began to scoop up the old woman's hair on to the top of her head, her fingers light and very gentle. "I want to see the picture you've done of me," she said.

"And how do you know about that?" Dora sounded so cross that Morag's spirits sank.

"The children told me about it. Please let me see it, Dora! Nobody every painted me before – not even at school!"

"Then you are asking for yourself!"

93

Morag finished doing her mother-in-law's hair. "I suppose I am."

"And it has nothing to do with Peggy's welfare? I thought not! But I should have thought you'd want to see it in private first, not at a party!" She turned round to look at Morag better. "You're a fool! Don't you see that if everyone is busy looking at my paintings, they won't be looking at you? Wear your dress, my dear, and be the belle of the ball for once! Wasn't that your first idea?"

Morag flushed. She couldn't deny that it had occurred to her that if Pericles should see others looking at her with appreciation he might take a second look himself.

"I wanted to show off Peggy too," she whispered.

Dora dismissed such nonsense with an earthy sniff. "My dear, I find it very irritating that you'll never admit to having a selfish bone in your body! All right, we've established that you want the triumph of having Pericles at your feet and so you bought the dress. What made you change your mind?"

Morag gazed at her in silence. Surely she hadn't been as brazen as that? "Not at my feet!" she gasped.

"Have I got the expression wrong?" Dora demanded. Morag shook her head. "Not that it matters! Are you afraid that Pericles will guess why you bought the dress?"

"N–no," Morag stammered.

"Then what is all this about the paintings?"

"I'm not much good at parties either!" Morag said. "And I don't speak Greek. I don't see how I'm going to shine at this party at all!"

"Then of course we shall show my paintings – and Peggy's too! Why on earth didn't you say so before?" Dora stood up and hugged Morag to her. "I didn't mean to say it now, but Pericles has had so much unhappiness, and a little bit of it was my fault. Now I want him to be happy with you and I will help you all I can, but you must help yourself a little too!" She cast Morag a look of mock despair. "You must *fight* for what you want, not hide behind the rest of us! How can Pericles notice you if you run away and hide?"

"He knows I'll give him anything he wants from me," said Morag.

Her mother-in-law looked more than a little exasperated. "Do you think he didn't have that with Susan? She was a perfect wife in many ways. In *every* way, except that she had no need of Pericles himself, and he knew it! This time, I had so hoped it would be different for him!"

Morag struggled to find the words that would reassure her, but as usual she was struck dumb when it came to what she wanted for herself. "I don't know how – " she began.

"Then you'd better find a way!" Dora snapped at her. She saw the tears in Morag's eyes and her expression relented a little. "Oh, come and see the portrait I've painted of you! When you've seen it, you may not want it to become public property. I can always put my others on show and keep this one as a wedding present for you and Pericles."

She led the way down the corridor from her room into which she had called Morag a few minutes before, to the small room at the other end that she had turned into a studio for herself. Morag had not been inside the room before and she stood now in the doorway, staring at the array of canvases that met her eye. How quickly Dora must work to have completed so many pictures so quickly! But then she saw her own features looking back at her and, fascinated, she studied the portrait of herself with a rising feeling of excitement.

Her mother-in-law had done the original drawing before she had married Pericles. She was sitting on the rough-hewn steps that led down to the sea and was wearing her oldest pair of jeans, a T-shirt that was none too clean, and the shell necklace that Perry had given her. The Beads of Nemesis, she called them to herself. They were a talisman, assuring her of the goddess's protection, and she would keep them all her days. But she had not thought before that

Pericles might need her services too, to compensate him for a marriage that had been less than perfect.

She took a step closer to the portrait. Apart from the casualness of her clothes, her hair was far from tidy and she had her hands clasped lightly about her knees. But it was the expression on her face that revealed exactly what she had been looking at when Dora had seen her. The desire in her eyes was a naked thing that made her embarrased to look at it, and her lips were damp as if she had just licked them, as if she couldn't wait for Pericles to turn round and kiss her. For there was no doubt that Pericles was standing just outside the canvas and that he, too, could see how much she wanted him.

"Has Pericles seen it?" she asked, her voice husky and not very well under control.

Dora studied the picture in a critical silence. She seemed to have forgotten all about the real Morag beside her.

"What did you say?" she asked at last.

"Has – has Pericles seen it?"

Dora grinned suddenly. "He'd be a fool if he hasn't! Oh, you mean the picture? No, not yet. I did it while you were both in England from a drawing I made of you the first day you were here. Do you want him to see it?"

"I don't know."

How could she want him to see it? It said far more than the words he had said he wanted from her!

Dora gave her a sardonic look. "Well, you have from now until the night of the party in which to make up your mind!"

Morag took a last look at the painting. "I have made up my mind!" She took a deep breath, hoping that she would somehow find the courage to go through with it. "I'd like it to be shown with the others."

CHAPTER SEVEN

THE gold dress was everything that Morag had hoped. When she had seen the children into their best clothes, and had helped Dora to dress her hair as she often did nowadays, she went to her own room and sank into the luxury of a hot bath, appreciating it all the more because it wasn't often that she was able to talk the maid into firing the boiler sufficiently for the water to be anything more than tepid when it came reluctantly out of the tap into the elaborately fitted bath. Pericles said hot water wasn't necessary in the summer in Greece. It was a theory that had surprised Morag, for she wouldn't have thought that her husband was the kind of man to believe in cold showers, or anything that wasn't the last word in comfort. But then she had to admit that she still knew very little about Pericles Holmes, let alone about his personal habits.

She went about her preparations for the party with an orderliness that would have amused her if she had not been keeping such a tight rein on her thoughts and emotions lest she turned tail and ran away long before any of the guests had arrived. It wasn't often that she paid much attention to her appearance, but tonight was different. Tonight, she had to build a brilliant shell between herself and her new family. It had been her own wish that Dora should show Pericles the portrait of herself for the first time in public, but she had determined that her real self would be as far removed from the vulnerable girl in the painting as it was possible for her to be.

Indeed, whenever she thought of her painted image her heart turned over with fright. How could she have looked at Pericles like that? He was bound to recognise the urgency of her need for him written clear in her eyes, and what would she do then? No matter what he said, she *couldn't* confess how often she had longed for him to take her in his arms and kiss her as he had kissed her that once before. Was that what he wanted her to put into words? Her cheeks flamed at the thought. Surely not! Surely he would know how impossible it was for her to ask – suggest – make him aware that her whole being cried out for him with an urgency that had first shocked her and, even now, made her wonder if he wouldn't despise her if he ever guessed how she felt about him. She had always pictured herself as being won and giving herself to some man in response to his need for her. She had never imagined that she might have to ask, or worse still to plead, with any man to make love to her. Yet it didn't look as though Pericles was ever going to make her his wife in fact as well as in name. He had said he wanted all the words, but if he were kind at all, he would surely accept the naked invitation his mother had caught on her face when she had been looking at him and thinking herself unobserved.

She spread the gold dress out on the foot of her bed and turned her attention to making up her face, a task that took all her attention because for once she wanted to look sophisticated and to bear the image of 'Swinging London' and, most of all, to put all the other women in the shade for the space of a few days. When she had finished she was herself rather surprised by the result. Her green eyes, as bright as emeralds, stared back at her in the glass, looking as mysterious as two green pools of light. She allowed her eyes to fall and was pleased by the shadowy effect of her long eye lashes. She had never thought of herself as beautiful, but tonight, she thought, she looked quite as well as she had ever seen Delia look. Excitement flooded through her veins, leaving a sensation of panic in its wake as she wondered if Pericles would notice and what he would do if he did.

Last of all, she dropped the golden dress over her head and smoothed down the skirt over her hips, marvelling at the elegant cut and the glowing brilliance of the material. She turned swiftly as the door-handle rattled briefly and opened to allow Pericles to walk into her room as calmly as if he did it every day – and with as little warning!

"I – I'm nearly ready," Morag faltered, wondering what he had come for.

"So I see."

The humour in his voice set the panic off again like fireworks through her blood. She glanced up at him, unaware of the appeal in her eyes. "Do you like it?" she asked him. His silence lent desperation to her next words. "You – did give it to me!"

"You look very lovely," he said at last, "but not quite the Morag I'm used to – "

"You *don't* like it!" she exclaimed in dismay. "Oh, Perry, why not? It's the most beautiful dress I've ever had!"

"Very splendid!" He smiled slowly. "I hope you remember whose wife you are this evening! Every eye – every masculine eye – will be following you in that!"

"Oh, do you think so?" Her eyelashes swept downwards. "I think I might rather like that!"

"Indeed?" he said dryly. "Well, keep your pleasure under control, if you can. You have no business attracting other men to want to make love to you, and I'm not the sort of man to stand by idly watching his wife flirt with other men!"

"Oh," she said. The excitement within her was almost unbearable. "Will you – will you flirt with me?"

"Do you want me to?"

She licked her lips "I don't know." Her eyes flashed up to his face and dropped again. "D-do you?"

"That would be telling," he drawled

"But Pericles" – she began.

Pericles raised his eyebrows. "Are you asking me to flirt with you, Morag?"

"No, no, of course not!" She smoothed down her skirts again and then stopped, thinking that he might think that she was trying to draw his attention to the very feminine line of the dress. "I wouldn't do that!"

He put a hand under her chin and forced her to look up at him. "Why not?"

"I'm not very good at it – and you might not want to!"

"Not very good at it? Oh, Morag! Don't let me catch you dallying with anyone else, that's all I ask! You'll regret it if you do!"

"Will I?" She tried to escape his restraining fingers. "I don't think you'd hurt me."

"Don't you?" The pressure of his fingers increased, though his thumb caressed her lips which trembled beneath his touch. "I hope you're right!"

She pulled herself together with an effort. "What could you do to me?" she dared him. She put a hand over his thumb, pulling it away from her mouth. "You'll smudge my lipstick!"

"I'm sorry," he said automatically. He didn't look sorry at all. On the contrary, he looked as sure of himself and as autocratic as she had ever seen him. "No, dammit, I'm not sorry at all! Who has a better right to smudge your lipstick anyway?"

"But not now!" she protested, hoping against hope that he would overrule her.

"No, not now," he agreed.

She winced, but he still didn't release her. "Please, Pericles," she whispered.

"Please what? Kiss you?"

Oh yes! Her heart thundered within her. "Please let me go."

He did so with a snap of his fingers. "Very well, but I meant what I said, and you would do well to remember that!"

Morag tried to hid her disappointment as best she may, making a play of looking at herself in the glass to see if she had to repair her make-up. But the tears in her eyes hardly allowed her to see her own reflection. Despair gripped her. The dress had made no difference! If it had Pericles would have kissed her whether she had asked him or not. He wouldn't have been able to help himself!

"I'm not likely to forget!" she muttered.

His eyes met hers in the looking-glass.

"See that you don't!" he said.

"Did you come only to threaten me?" she asked him.

"No, I came to see if you wanted me to zip you up again – and give you this!" He put his hand into his pocket and drew out something that flashed as green as her eyes. "Jade for a jade," he murmured. "I thought it would go with the dress." He made to put it on for her, but she took a quick step away from him, determined that he shouldn't touch her again. With a gesture of impatience, he put his hands on her shoulders and pulled her against him. "Stand still," he commanded her.

She could feel his breath on the back of her neck, then the coldness of the jade against her skin as he fastened the chain for her. She shut her eyes, wondering what he would do if she were to turn in his arms and thank him in the one way she longed to do, with her lips – Then she felt the kiss on the nape of her neck and she had no choice in the matter, for he had turned her to face him and his mouth descended on hers with a force that lit the short fuse of her own desire and she was kissing him as much as he was kissing her.

"We must go and meet our guests," he said at last, putting her from him.

Morag nodded her head. "I suppose so." She half laughed, half sobbed. "Thank you for this, Pericles." She fingered the jade pendant, her cheeks pink. "I think I like my shells better, though – my beads of Nemesis."

He shrugged. "I think I do too," he said, "though possibly not for the same reason."

She looked her enquiry, busily putting on some more lipstick, but Pericles only smiled and shook his head at her.

They went together in the sitting room. To Morag, it seemed the room was already filled to capacity and she was glad of Pericles' support as he put his arm lightly around her waist and introduced her to his many Greek friends. More of them spoke English than she thought possible, and after a while she began to enjoy herself, finding that almost everyone there was prepared to like her, and not only for her husband's sake, but because they found her likeable for herself. Morag, quite unaccustomed to being the centre of attraction, found it a heady experience.

Not even Takis, annoying as she found him, could disturb her new-found serenity. She took a step closer to Pericles, but she didn't really mind when Takis manoeuvred her away from his side and over to the other side of the room where he could speak to her without being overheard by Pericles.

"You look beautiful," he congratulated her. "You see what good taste I have. Didn't I advise you that that is the dress for you?"

"Did you?"

"You know I did! Though I didn't know that you had such a beautiful pendant that would set it off to perfection!"

"Pericles gave it to me, he gave it me just now."

Takis grinned at her. "So the dress had the desired effect?"

Morag shook her head. "I – I didn't want him to give me anything."

Takis took her hand and raised it to his lips. "Not many people would believe that, but I do. I am very hurt, Morag, here in my heart. When you first came here, you looked at me with your green eyes and I thought you liked me very well, but all the time you were planning the conquest of another!"

102

Morag smiled. "It was he who conquered me," she murmured.

"No, not yet," Takis contradicted her. "When that happens, I shall totally give up hope. But until then I shall try to do to you what you have done to me!"

"I haven't done anything to you!"

"You have stolen my heart!" Takis returned, a gleam of laughter in his eyes. "I will revenge myself on you for that!"

"Will you?" Morag drew herself up, though she was still smiling. "Pericles will protect me from anything you can do!"

The teasing quality disappeared from Takis' voice. "Like he did Susan? He made no pretence to defend her!"

Morag felt suddenly cold. She had forgotten all about Susan for the moment.

"Did she need his protection?" she asked.

"She was his wife too. He allowed her to do as she pleased. He did not protect her by calling her to heel – "

"Perhaps he trusted her," Morag put in.

Takis favoured her with a glittering smile. "Would you like to be so trusted?" He laughed softly. "Not by Pericles, you would not!"

She was saved from having to answer by someone coming up behind her. She looked around and saw that it was Pericles. She turned to him at once. "Did you want me?" she asked.

"My mother is getting ready to show her paintings. She wants you to help her to arrange them." He looked curiously at her. "She tells me our wedding present is among them."

Morag cast him an unconscious look of appeal. "Only if you like it," she began to explain. "You may not want it!"

"I shall hardly hurt my mother's feelings by saying so!" he said dryly.

"No," Morag agreed. "But Dora herself said you might not like it. She wouldn't want to hang it if you don't!"

Pericles put his hand on her upper arm, pushing her

forcibly through the door and out into the hall. "Never mind that just now," he bade her grimly. "What was Takis saying to you?"

"Nothing!"

"I prefer you keep it that way! You have nothing to say to him, no matter how he flatters you and makes eyes at you – "

"He doesn't mean anything by it!"

"Doesn't he?" Pericles' hand tightened about her arm until she uttered a cry of protest. "I warn you again, Morag, if you want to flirt with anyone, flirt with me!"

"Why should I?" she demanded, rubbing her arm.

He said something in Greek which she didn't understand, though she thought she recognised the words *'yinéka mou'* which she knew to mean 'my woman'.

"You don't own me!" she said.

He laughed and pushed her before him into his mother's studio. "Don't tempt me, Morag."

Tempt him? She didn't think she could, otherwise she would have done so this long time past. Sometimes she thought she was fixing herself in his mind and heart, but mostly she knew better and that as far as he was concerned she was no more than someone he had found to look after his children. Of course he liked to keep things normal on the outside, but it seemed she was alone in longing for love. He was able to do without it.

"Well, you don't own me!" she said with spirit. "If I like Takis, I don't see why I shouldn't talk to him all I want to!" She very nearly added 'So there!' but was prevented by the look on his face. It served him right, she thought rebelliously, to be a little less sure of her. Perhaps he would notice her more if she stood up to him.

She looked uncertainly at him and looked away again as quickly.

"Indeed?" he said coldly.

"As a matter of fact," she answered, "as a matter of fact I

don't care for Takis – "

"Then you don't need to talk to him?"

"N-no, though I can't ignore him completely. He is your cousin and, seeing he's staying in the same house – " She broke off. "Perry, I do try not to be alone with him!"

"Try a little harder!" he advised, his voice tinged with ice. "I mean what I said about that young man. You're my wife, Morag, not his. See that you remember it!"

She blinked. "You have very Greek ideas sometimes," she said. "But I'm not Greek. You ought to remember that!"

The coldness left his face. "What do you mean by that?" he drawled, giving her an amused look.

"I mean I have a mind of my own!" she answered defiantly, taking a grip on herself. It wasn't the moment she would have chosen to have a row with him, but if he wanted it that way, she wouldn't baulk at obliging him. Her eyes glinted dangerously, reflecting the fearful excitement that still clutched at her stomach. "I don't take orders!" she added for good measure.

"You'll take mine," he answered. He still looked amused, and that added a fatal spark to her temper.

"Why should I?" she demanded.

"Because," he said quietly, "in the last resort, we both know that you would rather please me than fight with me. You may not be Greek, but you'll take your lead from me and be pleased to have it so. Don't be silly, Morag! Would you rather have it the other way round?"

Fortunately for Morag, she escaped having to answer because her mother-in-law came rushing into the room, her hair standing on end, and looked with surprise at the two of them.

"What are you doing in here?" she asked Pericles. "I keep telling everyone that I'm not going to show the paintings in here! The light isn't right. All I need is a little help in moving the few that I want seen into the other room. If you carry these ones, Morag can manage the one with its face to the wall, and I'll bring in any others I've decided on while you're shifting those."

Pericles grinned. "Which one is our wedding present?"

Dora shrugged her shoulders. "We'll leave you to guess," she turned on Morag, running a hand through her hair, thus making it look wilder than ever. "It'd serve you right if Pericles humbled your pride for you in front of all those people!" Her expression softened at the look on Morag's face. "You look beautiful in that dress, my dear. I'll have to paint you again in that one day, but not until you've found yourself." Her enthusiasm grew as she thought about it. "Yes, it will be a splendid counterpart to the first one! I'll give them both to you!"

"So that's what our wedding present is," Pericles remarked.

"But you're not to look at it yet!" Morag put in hastily. She was surprised to hear that her voice sounded quite normal. Even so, she couldn't quite bring herself to look at her husband in case he, too, should know what Dora had meant both by her finding herself and by the hope that Pericles would humble her pride. Dear God, it was uncomfortable enough to be in love with a man without having to tell him so *in words*, when one had no idea if he even liked in return, let alone felt any of the hurricane of emotion in which she found herself.

"Why not?" Pericles asked.

She made no answer but turned her attention to struggling to lift the heavy canvas to take it into the other room.

"Here, let me have it!" said Pericles, taking it forcibly away from her. He turned it round and placed it back against the wall, standing well back and taking a long, thoughtful look at the painting.

Even Dora stood quite still awaiting his verdict. Morag's eyes went straight to the painted image of herself. Perhaps it wasn't as revealing as she had remembered it. And, if it was, perhaps Pericles wouldn't notice the naked invitation in her eyes, or the strength of her desire as she looked quite obviously at him. The silence stretched on and Morag longed for the floor to open and swallow her up! Couldn't he say something, *anything* at all?

But then he did speak and she wished just as passionately that he hadn't. "I didn't think anyone else had seen her like that," he said.

"Like what?" Morag asked in a whisper. She cleared her throat. "Like what?" she said again.

His eyes swept over her face, but without the tenderness she had been hoping to find in them. "As though you wanted to be loved," he said frankly.

The hot colour stormed up her face. "I don't! I mean your mother is a very clever artist. I was just the model –"

"Come," said Dora, "we must take the paintings into the other room. Peggy has done a sketch of Morag also. Perhaps Pericles will find more to like in that likeness of you."

"I like this one," said Pericles. "But I'd prefer it not to have a public viewing tonight. It is not a view I want other men to have of my wife!"

"Oh, arrogant!" Morag began, feeling a good deal safer by his decision. "Just because you think – "

"So would any man!" he retorted.

She turned away from him. "But you do like it?" she asked.

"Yes – " He cut himself off as he heard footsteps coming towards them. "Ah, Takis, have you come to help carry the paintings?"

The young Greek looked round the room, his eye falling on the painting of Morag. "Very pretty!" he commented. He gave her a wicked look, his smile wide and innocent. "Who were you looking at, *pedhi*? Ah, but I remember now when you sat there and dreamed your dreams! You were looking at me, Takis Kapandriti!"

Morag wanted to deny it, but there were no words that

107

came to her. She struggled vainly to defend herself when all she wanted to do was run away and hide. She owed that much to Pericles! She had to say something! This time she couldn't let them think what they liked about her. This time it was Pericles who would suffer.

"I remember it well too," she said in a small voice. She clenched her fists and drove herself on relentlessly. "Pericles had just said I'd never be free – " But her husband wasn't even listening. He had picked up a pile of paintings and had walked out of the room.

Morag thought the party was going on for ever. It was time the children were in bed, she thought, and wondered if they would think her very officious if she suggested that they should take themselves off. Peggy was flushed with success from the praise she had received from her drawings and probably wouldn't mind too much, but Kimon was deep in conversation with a man Morag had not previously noticed. Judging by the boy's absorbed expression they were talking about coins. Any moment now and Kimon's precious Spartan 'cartwheel' would be passed from hand to hand, while he told them yet again why it was so heavy and why it was made of nothing more valuable than iron.

But, rather to her surprise, the children were glad to go and disappeared without a murmur. Perhaps they had known that the party was about to break up anyway and knew they weren't going to miss anything. Morag stood beside her husband and mother-in-law and wished them all goodnight to their friends, a fixed smile on her face. She knew now that she would never be happy with Pericles, and she thought the knowledge would destroy her, so badly did it hurt to know that he would never love her but that, on the contrary, he wasn't even sufficiently interested to know that it was he who held her heart and not – nor ever could be – Takis Kapandriti!

What a relief it was to divest herself of her golden dress

108

and to put on a cotton nightdress and a thin, filmy negligée that barely covered her at all. She went to take a last look at the children and found Kimon in tears.

"Morag, I've lost my coin! I took it into the garden to see what it looked like by moonlight and I dropped it on the path, and I can't find it!"

She put her arms round him and hugged him tight. "I'll have a look," she offered.

"But supposing you don't find it?"

"I shan't go to bed until I do!" she assured him. "I'll give it to you in the morning. Don't worry about it now!"

But her confidence took a dive when she had crawled up and down the path on her hands and knees and still hadn't found the coin. She didn't even mind when she heard Takis humming to himself as he came up from looking at the sea and found her there, stopping only a couple of feet away from where she was kneeling.

"Don't just stand there!" she said crossly. "Help me look for Kimon's coin! He'll be desolate if he's lost it!"

Takis obediently fell on his knees beside her and began feeling round for the coin. "Why do you make yourself the servant of these children?" he asked her.

She answered deliberately. "What other role have I here?"

"*Morag!*"

With a sinking heart she knew that Pericles had already seen her and, worse still, that he had seen Takis with her. "Kimon's lost his coin!" she explained.

Pericles bent down until his eyes were practically on the same level as hers. "I warned you, Morag," he bit out at her. He lifted her bodily to her feet. "Go into the house at once!"

She looked down at the inadequate negligée she was wearing and hurried to obey him. He came after her almost immediately, catching up with her in the hall.

"While you are my wife, you will not entertain your lovers at my front door!" he told her.

109

"But I wasn't! I was looking for Kimon's coin!"

For a long moment he stared angrily at her, then he opened the door to his bedroom and thrust her inside before him. "If you want to be loved," he said tautly, "you can make up your mind to be loved by me!"

She backed away from him, almost falling on to the bed behind her. "But I didn't go out to meet Takis – I *wouldn't*!"

His hands slipped her negligée off her shoulders, ignoring her protests. He pushed her back against the pillows, his lips taking possession of hers with a fierceness that took her breath away. She made a last effort to prevent him from taking her more firmly into his arms, but her own need to give way to him was too strong for her.

"Oh, Pericles!" she breathed.

She felt him against her and she clung to him, welcoming his warm hands against her flesh. She didn't care how it had happened, she didn't care what happened afterwards, but to belong utterly to her husband was the fulfilment of everything she had ever dreamed of for herself.

Pericles was no longer beside her when she awoke. She started up, afraid that he had left her alone, but then she heard him splashing in the bathroom and knew he would soon be back, and that she would have to say something to him when he did. The door swung open and he came through it, his eyes brilliant as he looked at her. Reddening despite herself, she looked away from him and her eye fell on Kimon's Spartan coin on the bedside table. She reached out for it, her heart pounding out a new, unfamiliar message within her.

"You found the coin!" she accused him. "You knew I was telling you the truth all the time!"

Pericles came over to the bed. He leaned over her, putting a hand on either side of her slim body.

"Yes, I knew," he said.

"Then – " She blushed vividly. "I think you might have

told me you knew," she said.

There was a curious look in his eyes and she found herself thinking how white and strong his teeth were, and that his mouth was every bit as strong and firm as it had felt against hers.

"Are you expecting an apology?" he asked her, the look in his eyes deliberately mocking. "I don't have to apologise for making love to my own wife!" he told her, as arrogant as she had ever seen him. "Not even to her!" he added. He bent his head and took an unhurried toll of her lips. "*Especially* not to her!"

CHAPTER EIGHT

PERICLES had gone out. Morag passed a restless half-hour trying to persuade herself that she didn't care where he had gone, but she failed dismally in this that she was all the more pleased to see her mother-in-law coming into the dining-room for her breakfast. Dora gave her a long, interested look as she sat down, smiling suddenly with all the warmth that made some people say she was the most charming woman they had ever met.

"You have a glow this morning, my dear. I think I shall have to paint you again like you are now. Perhaps Pericles would like it better. Positively complacent!" Her smile lit her eyes and died again. "It has happened to other women before, you know!"

Morag was getting used to Dora's odd, slanting shafts of humour. "But never to me!" she said. She eyed her mother-in-law across the table. "Nobody can take that away from me!"

"Why should anyone want to?" Dora asked dryly.

"Always before, someone has."

"Delia?"

Morag nodded. "Did Perry tell you about her?"

"Not really," Dora said with disinterest. "I think he mentioned her name once."

"Most men prefer her."

"Oh? I thought she had always been jealous of you? Didn't she try and take your young man away from you?"

Morag stared at her. "How did you know?"

"Kimon told me," Dora said simply. "He had heard you and Pericles talking about it. Children hear far more than they are ever meant to. I can't say that young man sounds much of a loss. Do he and Delia intend to marry?"

"No," Morag said. "David is dead. He was killed in a car crash."

Dora yawned. "I suppose she was driving?"

Morag maintained an uncomfortable silence. It was odd to think about David now. She knew now that she had never loved him, and that her liking for him had been rather uncertain, bred of habit and the comfortable certainty that sooner or later they would come together in a more permanent relationship as other people did.

"Well?" said Dora.

"I never thought of it before," Morag wondered at herself, "but Delia never did have any particular boy-friend of her own. Do you suppose that was why she wanted David?"

"Quite likely!"

"David wasn't really in love with me. He took one look at Delia and that was that. I might just as well not have existed!"

"You must have been very young to have minded so much," Dora commented. "He sounds a very dull young man, with not much understanding of life if he thought this Delia would suit him better. I hope you told him so?"

"Well, no," Morag confessed.

"But you decided he should have what he wanted?"

"If it was Delia he wanted."

"I must say you were quite as stupid as Pericles says you were! It was she who killed him, I suppose?"

Morag bowed her head. "Did Pericles tell you that too?"

"Pericles tells me nothing! And Kimon, who would tell me, did not know that! But now you are not so young and silly, *ne*? You gave this young man away, but that was an extravagance of youth! You would not give your present happiness away so easily to your sister, or to anyone else. Have you told Pericles that?"

Morag avoided the question. "She's my stepsister."

Dora made an exasperated gesture. "It is only an excuse to say you are shy!" she muttered. "I hope he beats you if you don't tell him very soon! It was bad enough that Susan should only tolerate what she should have seized with gratitude, but with you it is quite different, and I am glad it should be so! I want my son to be loved above all else! Whether he in turn loves you is a matter of indifference to me. It matters to me only that you should love him and that he should know it!"

"I love Pericles very much," Morag said simply.

"Tell that to him!" Dora retorted.

"How do you know I haven't?" Morag burst out.

"Have you?"

"No." Morag wished she had cultivated the art of telling lies better and were not quite so naturally truthful. It was true enough that she had not told Pericles anything, but surely, sometimes, actions spoke louder than words? She sighed, knowing that it was the words that Pericles wanted, and words never came easily to her, and were now harder than ever to find when they mattered so much. She lifted her head. "Not that it's any business of yours!" she added to her mother-in-law.

Dora gave her a quick look of appreciation. "Quite right!" she applauded. "It would have been much easier for you if you had a proper honeymoon away from us all. I have tried to keep out of it, my dear, but it's a bit difficult when we are all in the same house and on top of one another the whole time. I apologise."

It was the last reaction that Morag had expected. "It doesn't matter," she said awkwardly. "I don't mind – much. Only don't hope for too much. Pericles only married me to look after the children. I can't – can't expect that he should want me to hang round his neck all the time!"

Dora frowned. "Don't be too unselfish!" she warned. There was a short silence while Morag digested this, and then the older woman went on casually, "By the way, I thought I might take the children out tonight. They want to see the Son et Lumière of the Acropolis, and I want them to see the Dora Stratou Theatre of Greek Dance. It's right that they should take a proper interest in their heritage. Would you care to come too?"

Morag looked as confused as she felt. "I don't know," she said. "Won't Pericles think it odd if we all go out without him?"

"Pericles is going out himself," his mother let fall. "He won't be back till very late, if at all."

It was typical, Morag thought, that she should be the last to know! "Where is he going?" she asked.

Dora smiled faintly. "In Greece a man often goes out alone and it's seldom that he tells his womenfolk where he's going. Pericles is no exception to that!"

"But he's only half Greek!"

"He is living here," Dora pointed out. "So I take it you will come with us?"

Morag nodded. "Thank you," she said. But she didn't feel like thanking anyone. Her pleasure in the morning was quite destroyed. She sighed and poured herself some more coffee, just as Kimon and Peggy came in from the beach.

"Did you find it? Morag, did you find my coin? Please say you did! I would have come back and helped you look, but I heard Daddy talking to you." His eyes grew round at the memory. "He sounded awfully angry!"

Morag's features took on a calmness she was far from feeling. What else had Kimon heard? Pericles' angry accusation that he wouldn't allow her to entertain her lovers at his front door? Really, it was quite impossible to hold a private conversation in this house!

"He found your coin," she said aloud.

"Daddy did? But he didn't spend any time looking for it at all—"

"He – he came upon it immediately!" Morag cut him off.

"Oh," said Kimon. "Well, I'm glad it's found. It's my
115

most precious possession in all the world. Do you think I should thank him?"

"Of course you should!" Peggy chimed in. "Wasn't it a super party last night? I thought I'd die when Grandma showed all my drawings with hers, but they didn't look too bad, did they? There was one man there who wanted to take one of them home with him, but Daddy said no. It was the drawing I did of you, Morag. Did you look at it properly?"

"It depends what you mean by properly," Morag teased her.

"I mean, did you think it looked like you?"

Morag had thought so. She had her head flung back and she was laughing. She had been surprised to find herself thinking that the girl in the picture was more than a little bit pretty. She was striking to look at, and quite different from the way she thought of herself.

"I suppose it does. I don't see myself very often – except in the looking glass."

"No, one doesn't," Peggy agreed. "I thought," she went on happily, "that Grandma was going to show the painting she did of you too. Why didn't you, Grandma? I think it's terribly good!"

A sudden bark of laughter escaped from Dora's throat. She put up a hand to her mouth as if to prevent if from happening again. "Daddy said no," she said dryly.

"*Daddy* did?" both children said together. "Why?"

"You'll have to ask him," Dora suggested, but her eyes were on Morag's flushed face and, underneath, she was still laughing. "Meanwhile, will you hurry up and finish your breakfast or we shall never get anything done today! Parties are all very well, but they do disorganise one so!"

Morag didn't see Pericles all day. Not that she would have known what to say to him if she had. She would have liked to have known, quite as much as the children, why he had refused to allow the man to take away Peggy's drawing of herself. Whichever way she looked at it, it seemed an odd thing to do. She wished with all her heart that she could think it was because he wanted it for himself, but she knew that to be an idle hope before she had even voiced it to herself. Why should he? All he had to do was ask Peggy to do another drawing of herself any time she chose.

It was not until they were all in Dora's car on their way to Athens that evening that she thought to ask Peggy who the man had been who had wanted the drawing.

"Adoni? He's a cousin of ours." Peggy stretched lazily. "He pretends to be Takis' twin, because they're almost the same age, but he isn't, of course. They aren't even brothers, though they've always done practically everything together. Kimon and I are the only real twins in the family!"

"I don't see why he should want a drawing of me," Morag went on worrying at the point. "I've never seen him before!"

Kimon looked kindly at her. "He would have given it to Takis," he explained as if her were speaking to a simpleton. "Takis said he wanted it to put it up in his room."

Morag gave him a quick glance. "Are you sure?"

Kimon nodded. "I don't suppose Takis really wanted it," he consoled her. "He probably thought it would annoy Daddy."

Morag suppressed a strong wish to strangle Takis and his cousin. If it had been anyone else but Kimon to say such a thing, she would have discounted it as his imagination, but Kimon was not given to fantasies and his lack of interest in the whole subject was made clear when he changed the subject back to his beloved coin, eagerly telling his grandmother that he was sure it was one of the best examples of Spartan coinage still extant in Greece.

But Morag could not forget what he had said as easily. For the first time she began to wonder in earnest about Susan, what she had been like, and whether she had really been in love with Takis. There had to be some reason why

117

Takis should want to hurt Pericles any way he could? Was it because he hadn't been as sure as he pretended to be that Susan had preferred him to her own husband? Oh well, no one could tell her that now. Just as she would never be able to ask David if Delia had only run after him because she had been unable to bear the fact that David preferred her stepsister. What unhappiness such conceit in one's own attraction could cause! Was that the sin that the ancient Greeks had called *hubris*, the crime of thinking that one could be master of one's own destiny, of presuming to think that one could take anything merely because one wanted it? Morag fingered the shells round her neck with a faint shiver. It was Nemesis whose duty it was to punish all such presumption. On whom would her vengeance fall next?

"I'm tired, Grandma!" Peggy complained, breaking into Morag's train of thought. "Why did we have to come tonight? I'm tired!"

"You slept late enough this morning," her grandmother told her.

"But I'm tired!"

"Hush," said Morag. "You can sleep afterwards."

"But not for ages! The Son et Lumière doesn't begin until nine o'clock!"

"Doesn't it?" Morag exclaimed. "But it gets dark much earlier than that!"

Dora compressed her lips together signifying her displeasure. "I thought you'd like to hear it in English. The children understand English better than any other language too. Also it fits in better with the Dora Stratou Theatre."

"You see," said Peggy, "we shan't get to bed before tomorrow! And I'm tired now!"

So was Morag! She wondered what time Pericles would be coming home and wished she had never agreed to come.

"Don't whine!" Kimon rebuked his sister. "You know

118

Daddy doesn't like it! He says it makes things worse if you whine – they take longer to live through!"

Morag began to feel sorry for her mother-in-law. Really it was too bad to have *three* reluctant guests on her hands! To make up for the children's lack of enthusiasm, she began to ask about the Greek dances they were going to see. "I seem to have heard of Dora Stratou –"

"Of course you have!" Dora snapped. "She's won all sorts of international prizes for her work." She turned her head so that the children also could hear what she was saying. "The Greek dance is one of the oldest in the world," she told them. "Much of it was lost at one time and all that there was to go on was the odd mention of it here and there in Homer. But Kyria Stratou has studied the representations of the old dances on ancient vases, on friezes, wherever they could be seen, and has faithfully revived them. The most interesting thing to my mind is that the Greek musical rhythms are based on the old poetic rhythms: 5/4, or 5/8, 7/8, 9/8, the very same metres that are to be found in the plays of Aeschylus, Euripides, and Sophocles. You can hear the same beat in the Byzantine music of the Orthodox Church if you listen for it."

Morag smiled at the children's blank faces, realising that they had not understood one word of their grandmother's introduction to the evening's entertainment. "I expect you'll like the costumes," she suggested, sounding more optimistic than she actually was.

Dora snorted her contempt at the very idea. "They must learn to use their eyes! Especially Peggy, if she is determined to paint anything worthwhile. She will do better if she considers where she may have seen the costumes and the musical instruments before. It may have been in a Byzantine fresco, or in a statue depicting one of the ancient gods, on a vase in the National Museum, maybe even on a Christmas card! One has to learn to relate the things one sees to other things. This is the secret of a good painting, or a good design. Sometimes I think it's the best basis for the whole of life!"

"But Grandpa didn't think so," Peggy said in bored tones.

"No," Dora was forced to agree in unnaturally subdued tones. "It's sometimes difficult to see any use in any of the arts. Your grandfather was an essentially practical man and he thought anything that didn't have an immediate practical use was a waste of time. I think he forgot that the soul can get hungry too!"

"Was he – was he like Pericles?" Morag heard herself asking.

Dora considered the question. "In some ways," she said. "He was a hard man, but he tried always to be gentle with me. I doted on him." She sighed. "I'd rather have him than my painting any day!"

Just as Morag would rather have Pericles than all the other gifts all the ancient gods put together could lavish on her. She rubbed her shells between her fingers in a quick, nervous movement. If Nemesis were real, would she think that Morag deserved Pericles? Somehow, Morag couldn't think so. She had so very little to offer him and someone like Pericles deserved only the best. She tilted her chin into an obstinate angle. Then she would have to become the best for him, because nobody else was going to have him!

The people who had just seen the Son et Lumiere performance in German were still coming out from the natural theatre that looked out and up at the rock of the Acropolis, surmounted by the Parthenon. Dora allowed the children to buy themselves some Coca-Cola, taking it for granted that Morag, like herself, would prefer to do without.

"The mosquitoes are bad at this time of year!" the older woman complained, slapping her arms. "Something ought to be done about them!"

Morag, who had suffered from various bites ever since

she had arrived in Greece, wondered if the season really made much difference. "They're at their worst at night. I wonder why?"

Dora shrugged. "One notices them more. Can you see the children anywhere? It looks as though we are at last moving."

Morag found the children with some difficulty and firmly anchored them to her by holding them both by the hand. She knew that they resented being treated as younger than they were, but she had no intention of losing them in the crowd that pressed all round them. "It won't be for long, just till we get inside," she told them.

Kimon blinked up at her. "We're not going inside," he corrected her. "It's an outside theatre."

"Well, it comes to the same thing," Morag retored. "I don't want to lose you and I don't want to get lost myself either!"

"You won't get lost!" he said scornfully.

"I hope not," she murmured.

She was glad they were sufficiently high up in the queue to be able to have a choice of seats. Dora selected the four seats she wanted with enormous care, making certain that the children could see before she sat down herself, her own shoulders sagging a little with fatigue. "Perhaps we shouldn't have come tonight," she said to Morag. "We're all tired!"

Morag smiled. "I find it rather exciting," she said. "Did you ever see anything more beautiful than the Acropolis, lit up like that? How fortunate Athens is to have such a monument right at the heart of the city. There's nothing like it anywhere else in the world, is there?"

"No," Dora said. "Compared to London, Paris, or Rome, or even Washington or New York, Athens is little more than a village. But give me my village every time! It is my home and I love it, like a woman loves a man, or a man a woman."

Morag was surprised to find that she felt a little bit the same way herself. She supposed it was because so much that was the history of Athens belonged to the whole European culture, and therefore everyone was more or less at home there. But she liked to think it was a little more than that. She wanted to think that Pericles had somehow conferred a citizen status on herself, that it was because of him that it was her home too.

Then the lights went out and the days of Pericles and the Athenian victory against the Persians at Marathon once more came alive before their eyes. It was, perhaps, rather a ragged history of that glorious era when the Parthenon had come into being, and Herodotus, the father of historians, had laboured to reveal the world he knew to itself, with an attempt at objectivity never before seen in the ancient world. The small gem of a temple, dedicated to victory, glowed with a great light as the messenger from Marathon brought the news of victory to the city, though nothing was said of the way the man had run, expiring as he whispered the glad tidings, or that this was the origin of the great marathon race that is still contested by long-distance runners to this very day.

Last of all came the voice of Athene, the grey-eyed goddess of wisdom who had given her name to the city and to whom the Parthenon was dedicated, and once again she lived among her people, Greeks and strangers, all of them who recognised her patronage that had brought to life this first of Europe's great civilizations, the first and in many ways the finest of them all.

Even the children were silent when the last trumpet died away and Athene's voice faded across the centuries and into oblivion. They rose with the others and scuffed the sides of their shoes on the gravel path as they left the auditorium.

"Funny," said Peggy, "but I'm not in the least bit tired now!"

Her grandmother unbent sufficiently to say that she was feeling more like enjoying herself too. "We haven't taken Morag out nearly enough," she said to both of the children. "Never mind, when her family comes out to visit us, we'll take them all to the Argolid, or Delphi. It's a long time since I saw the theatre at Epidaurus myself."

Morag gave Dora a quick glance.

"Mmm. That stepsister of yours, whatever her name is. Didn't Pericles tell you? She sent a telegram saying that she was coming – the only trouble is she didn't say when!"

"But she can't come here!"

"Why not?" Dora sounded amused. "I suppose Perry didn't tell you about her because he only heard this morning. Your father wanted her gone for a while, or so she said."

"My father?" Morag exclaimed. "Now that I can't believe!"

Dora shrugged, fitting herself into the front seat of her car. "Well, we can hardly refuse to have her with us, dear. Perhaps it won't be for too long!"

Morag pressed her point. "Couldn't you say it isn't convenient right now?"

"No, I couldn't." Dora hesitated. "Pericles did say she was to stay as long as she wants to," she said then. "I'm sorry, dear."

Morag's spirits sank. "I don't believe that my father would have asked her to leave home. He adores her – just like her mother!"

"Well, as to that, I couldn't say, but I think I shall be quite interested to see this stepsister of yours. If she's as lovely as you say, I may like to paint her. What do you think?"

Morag made a face and then pretended that she hadn't as she caught sight of the children watching her. "I wish she wasn't coming!" she declared.

"Don't you like her?" Peggy demanded.

"She's my stepsister!" Morag said.

"That's no answer!" Kimon reproved her. "Is she silly or something?"

Morag affected some amusement she did not feel. "Very silly!" she agreed.

Kimon gave her a very grown-up look. "I'll be able to see for myself if she comes to stay." He smiled suddenly, in the same audacious way as his father did. "If you don't like her," he said, "I don't suppose we shall either."

It was only a short drive to the Dora Stratou Theatre in the Philopappou area. Once again Dora had selected their seats with immense care. She herself sat well forward, her eyes never leaving the colourful figures as they wove in and out of the various patterns of dance on the stage. Morag found it almost as much fun to watch her as to watch the dancers. Later on, she supposed, her mother-in-law would reproduce what she had seen in paint. Almost Morag could envy her gift, for it must be wonderful to be so absorbed in any creative activity. Then, fleetingly, she remembered how Dora had said she would willingly not paint if she could have her husband back, and she wondered if Pericles was home yet, and her heart missed a beat as she thought of the moment when she would see him again. If she only knew what he would expect from her –?

The dancing came to a sudden end and Dora bounced out of her seat, intent on getting the children home as quickly as possible. "You're to go straight to bed the moment we get home!" she bade them. "Morag too! She looks like a little ghost, especially under these lights."

There was no sign of Pericles at the house. Morag went to her room and undressed slowly. Perhaps, if she took a bath, Perry would be home by then? But Pericles wasn't, and, finding she couldn't sleep, she slipped into bed and tried to read her book, turning the pages every now and then, but taking in nothing of the story.

She was still reading when the door opened and Pericles

came in. She started, smiling nervously at his inscrutable face.

"My wife sleeps in my bed," he said. "I thought I'd made that clear last night."

Morag's fingers tightened round the spine of the book. "I prefer my own room," she murmured.

He raised his eyebrows thoughtfully. "Come on, Morag."

She pulled the bedclothes more closely about her. "I'm not coming!" she managed.

She scarcely saw his hand as he whipped the sheet away from her, but she felt the hard strength of his arms all right as he scooped her off the bed and on to her feet beside him. Pericles opened the door and bowed politely to her. "After you, Mrs. Holmes!"

She cast him a swift look through her eyelashes and lowered her eyes hastily at the unyielding look on his face. She picked up her negligée and, when he took it away from her, began to search for her slippers, only to have them removed from her nerveless fingers as well. She hugged her book to her, but that too joined the growing pile of discarded articles on the bed.

"Morag," he said at last, "if you don't come now, I'll turn you over my knee and smack you."

She turned a scarlet face to him. "I *hate* you!" she declared. "Do you hear me? I hate you!"

"Do you?" He put a hand on her shoulder, allowing his fingers to trail down her back, caressing her even while he drew her inexorably to him. "If you want to fight," he said in her ear, "you can fight me decently in bed, with no holds barred, like a man and woman should. Then, when you've had enough –"

She clung to him, not trusting her knees to hold her up. "You can't make me!"

He held her closer still, running his lips across her eyes and slowly down to her mouth, kissing her so lightly that she stifled a sob and tried to hide her face from him.

"I think I can make you," he said. "You are my woman and I'll make love to you when and how I please, no matter what you think!" He put a hand on her heart. "You need loving, Morag. Why won't you admit it?"

She hid her face in his shoulder. "If you *asked* me," she pleaded, "but you don't care what I think or feel! You had no reason to be angry last night, no reason to – to take it out on me!"

He dragged his fingers through her hair, pulling her head back and kissing her mouth again. "If I had thought you were playing with Takis in earnest, I should not have been so gentle with you, my Morag! And you would not be standing here arguing with me now! Be grateful that I did believe you! Are you going to pretend that you didn't want me to make love to you?" He gave her a little shake. "Well?"

She tried hard to tell him how much she wanted him, but the words would not come. If he only loved her a little, but she knew better than that!

"I know I'm your wife and – and –" She swallowed. "Oh, Perry, I want to be more than just a convenience –"

His laughter shattered what little pride she had left. "Not a very convenient convenience, as you won't come to bed," he teased her. "Come on, Mrs. Holmes, you may as well bow to the inevitable. Will you walk, or shall I carry you?"

She gave him a speaking look that lost most of its sting as she gave way to the pressure of his arms with something very like relief. He pushed her hair back from her face, running his thumb down the line of her jaw. "Is it war or peace?" he asked her.

The hot colour flooded her cheeks. "Peace." Her eyes fell before the look in his. "An armistice until – if that's what you want?"

"All right." He looked down at her, his eyes quizzical. "An armistice it will be. But one day I shall demand a total

126

surrender, *karthiá mou*, and there will be no half measures then! You'll tell me everything I want to know before I sign a final peace treaty with you!"

"But you know –"

"I want the words," he said very gently. "Is that so much to ask?"

She couldn't answer him. If she could have found the words, she would have said them there and then, but how could she when he had not offered her a single word of love? And it was that knowledge which brought a droop to her shoulders and a slowness to her steps as she preceded him out of the room, down the corridor into his bedroom, and finally under the hand-embroidered covers of his bed.

CHAPTER NINE

"PERRY, I want to learn Greek."

Her husband looked amused. "Are you asking my permission?"

"Not exactly," Morag said. "It's more in the nature of a warning. I don't like being called names that I don't understand –" His laughter made her hesitate, but then she went on: "I don't like your laughing at me either!"

His eyes took on a wicked brilliance. "There seems to be a great deal that you don't like this morning?"

"You never take me seriously!" she complained. "It's not my fault that I can't speak Greek!"

"No," he agreed. "Why don't you ask for a translation?"

"Because you only speak Greek at the most inconvenient moments! You know very well what I mean!" she continued repressively.

"Indeed I do!"

"Well, I don't like it!"

"Poor Morag," he drawled. "I don't remember calling you anything very dreadful, however. What would you like me to call you?"

"I don't know," she said. But she did know. She wanted to be called 'darling', and 'beloved', and 'his much beloved wife'.

"Then you'll have to put up with my Greek names for you!" He slid out of bed, looking down at her. "*Karthiá mou! Yinéka mou! Agapi mou!*"

"Ah," she said, "I know what *yinéka* means, it means woman!"

"And wife!"

She ignored that. "And *karthiá*?"

He grinned at her. "*Karthiá*? It means heart!"

"Oh," said Morag, suddenly breathless.

"You see," he said, pressing home his advantage, "it's nothing very bad, is it? I don't think you have much to complain about."

She sat up, hugging her knees, tossing up in her mind if she would also ask him what *agapi mou* meant. She decided against it, realising he was still staring down at her and seemed to be expecting something from her.

"You look doubtful," Pericles said dryly.

"I – I didn't kn–know," she stammered. "It could have meant anything!"

"Well, now you do know, I hope I have your permission to call you anything I please, in Greek or English, or any other language?"

Morag licked her lips, trying to drag her eyes away from his. He looked so splendid, so dark and immovable, so very much the master of the situation!

"I suppose so," she said.

She thought she was going to drown in the brightness of his eyes and that she wouldn't be able to care that he didn't love her, but would have to confess her own love for him and beg him to be kind to her. But then another matter came to mind and the moment passed. Her eye kindled with remembered indignation.

"How long have you known that Delia is coming here? I think you might have told me, instead of leaving it to your mother!" she sighed. "Why has she got to come here anyway?"

"She's a member of your family."

Morag's eyes flashed. "I'd prefer her not to come." she said mutinously.

He sat down on the bed beside her. "And I prefer that she does come. I have no wish to be thought inhospitable by your parents."

"She's not my real sister," Morag said. "Surely, if I don't

want her here –"

Pericles put a hand behind her head. "Can you give me a good reason why she shouldn't come?" he asked. "Come, Morag, I'm not unreasonable! Tell me why you don't want her here and perhaps I'll agree with you and tell her not to come."

"Isn't it enough that I don't want her?" She sounded almost as desperate as she felt. With Delia in the same house as Pericles, what chance would Morag have to make him fall in love with her?

His fingers stroked her neck. "No, I don't think so. I want your family to feel free to visit you whenever they wish to. Besides, when you see her again, I don't think you'll find you dislike her half as much as you used to. She's really a very attractive young woman!"

She sighed, hating to have another clash of wills with him so soon. "As your wife, I consider I have the right to have some say in whom we invite here," she burst out, wishing that she could sound as cool and logical as he did.

"As my wife," he retorted, "you will do as I think best – or take the consequences!"

"But that's barbaric!"

"Isn't it?" he agreed calmly. "Very Greek!" He pulled her hair gently, smiling straight into her eyes. "It won't do you any harm to have Delia here for a while. She can give you a hand with the children and give you a chance to have some time to yourself."

"Just because you say so?" she demanded. "Well, I won't –"

"You haven't much choice. She's coming, and that's that." He pulled her hair again, rather less gently. "Unless you have a good reason as to why she should stay away?"

She shook her head miserably. "She'll make trouble!"

"Then you'll have to cope with her when she does," he answered quietly. "If you care enough to put a spoke in her wheel, instead of giving way to her!"

Her eyes widened. "Why can't you give way to me?" she complained. "Only this once! It can't mean very much to you whether she comes or not."

"Ah, but it does!" He pushed her back against the pillows, studying her mouth with an interest that made her catch her lower lip between her teeth and avert her eyes. "Besides," he added, so softly that she couldn't be sure he had said it, "I like it when you're subservient and anxious to please me, and very, very feminine – like now!" His lips took hers with an insolent freedom that made it very clear what was her place in his scheme of things. She tried to twist away, but his hold on her hair made her cry out. Instantly she was free. "Did I hurt you?" he asked. "Morag, you shouldn't fight me!"

"I don't!" she snapped. "I'm not bossy like you!"

"*Bossy*?" His concern dissolved into laughter. "Because I won't let you have your way over Delia?"

"Because you *never* let me have my own way!"

He leaned on his elbow, putting out a hand to touch her face, tracing the line of her lips with his finger. "I will when you really know what you want," he promised. "At the moment you still haven't the courage of your convictions to dare all because only one thing matters to you. So you might as well go my way until you find your tongue, *karthiá mou*, because I know exactly what I want!"

Her lips trembled against his finger and her own hands came up round his neck to bury themselves in the virile black hair at his neck. "Pericles –" She shut her eyes and swallowed convulsively. Didn't he know how his touch awakened her own need for him?

"Well, go on, then," he said. "Why don't you ask me to kiss you?"

Her eyes flew open and she turned away from him. "I – I can't!" she said.

"Then you haven't any grievance because it's I who command you, *agapi mou*, for I can, and will, take your

131

kisses when I want them! With or without your consent," he added for good measure. He kissed her ear. "If you were honest you'd admit you were glad to have it that way, because you like my kisses, don't you?" He turned her face to his. "Don't you?"

"Yes, yes, *yes*!" She was almost in tears with frustration and, at that moment, she thought she disliked him more than anyone she knew. Then his mouth came down on hers and she melted into his arms in an agony of love for him. It was an unfair advantage he had, she thought while she could think at all, for he could rouse in her this delicious ecstasy at will, whereas she couldn't even find the words to beg him to kiss her again.

"There's a letter for you, Morag." Dora looked curiously at her daughter-in-law, but she said nothing. "Aren't you going to open it?"

"It's from Delia!"

"All the more reason to find out what she has to say." She smiled, revealing all the warm charm of which she was capable. "Do open it! I've been sitting here looking at it for nearly an hour, wondering if she's changed her mind and decided not to come after all. Even the children were up before you this morning!"

"Yes, I'm sorry. I thought they'd sleep late."

"They did!" Dora rejoined. "Only not so late as you did. I'd have brought you your breakfast in bed, but Pericles said you were to be left to sleep it out." She raised a sardonic eyebrow. "In my day it was the wife who guarded her husband's rest, not the other way round. Have you been finding the children too much for you, my dear?"

"N–no," Morag said.

"Wait until you have three or four to cope with! Kimon and Peggy are of an age when they can mostly look after themselves, but it's a different matter when they are babies!"

Morag gave her a confused look. "I don't know what

132

you're talking about."

"My dear girl, what do you think? Oh, don't bother to tell me that it's none of my business, because Perry has already done that! He actually said he wanted to have you to himself for a while! I think that's a very good sign, don't you? He looked so *happy* this morning! Just what I'd always hoped for him!"

But that wasn't because he loved her! Morag protested silently. It was because he didn't love her! He didn't want children while there were no solid foundations to their marriage. Who would? He might find someone he liked better than herself and he wouldn't want to feel guilty about leaving her and starting again with someone else. He was bound to prefer somebody else sooner or later. Someone like Delia, for instance. Someone who was gay and beautiful and very, very sure of her own attractions!

Morag turned her stepsister's letter over in her hand, trying to focus on the bright, purple ink in which the address was written. *Mrs. Pericles Holmes.* Her heart turned right over within her. Was that her? Pericles had called her Mrs. Holmes, but somehow that was quite different from Mrs. *Pericles* Holmes! That made her seem a part of him, such as she longed to be.

She tore open the envelope and pulled out the letter inside. It was seldom that Delia bothered to put pen to paper. She far preferred the telephone as a means of communication, and Morag could imagine that it must have been her father who had put his foot down this time or she would surely have rung through to Greece with as little thought as she rang up the people next door.

"Dear Morag," she read. "I don't suppose it makes any difference to you when I arrive, so I shall turn up when I'm ready. Everyone has been very cross ever since you left, and were crosser still when I said I intended visiting you. But I *liked* Pericles, and why should you mind if I come and look him up? You're safely married to him! Anyway, I'm

133

coming whether you want me to or not, because your father has been very odd lately and I don't want him to think we're less than good friends. Have you been telling him anything? Ma thinks you may have had a heart-to-heart when you were here getting married. It wouldn't be wise if you were to turn him against me, you know. Just thought I'd warn you! See you soon, Delia."

"May I read it?" Dora asked.

Morag coloured. "I'd rather you didn't," she murmured. "Delia says lots of things she doesn't mean –"

Dora held out an imperious hand. "If you want me for an ally while she's here, I may as well know the worst."

"All right," Morag said reluctantly. "It doesn't say anything anyway. I mean, it doesn't say anything much. It worries me about my father, though. He's always adored Delia and she could never do any wrong in his eyes."

"What about her mother?"

"She preferred Delia too. Delia was her own daughter and they're very – very alike!"

Dora came to the end of the letter and flung it down on to the table in front of her. "What could you have told your father about her?" she demanded.

"Nothing very terrible. It was always I who got into scrapes and had to be rescued from them. Delia never did anything wrong. Anything I could tell my father would have been my fault, far more than hers!"

Dora's eyes met hers. "Have you told Pericles?"

"He knows," Morag admitted.

"Then we needn't worry! Let her come and do her worst!" Dora wrinkled her nose fastidiously. "I don't think I'm going to like her. You can congratulate yourself, Morag Grant, in having a united family behind you! I thought you rather negligible when you first arrived, yet you have all of us eating out your hand: me, Kimon, Peggy – even Pericles! I wonder how you do it?"

Morag was absurdly pleased by her mother-in-law's
134

praise. "I like you all," she said, "and I want you to like me."

Dora chuckled. "Especially Pericles! No, don't bother to deny it. Even Kimon recognises that Pericles is the sun, the moon, and the stars to you. *Quite* different from Susan!" she added on a note of satisfaction. She looked back at Delia's letter. "I think we'll put her in your old room. It's nicer than the other spare room, which is smaller and rather hot at this time of year."

Was it her "old room" already? Morag supposed it was, although most of her things were still there, in the wardrobe and in the chest of drawers. It would be a good excuse to move in properly to the room she now shared with Pericles, she thought, knowing that she would never have found the courage to do so without such an excuse. It would also mean that there would be no going back there herself, and that, too, might have its advantages.

Dora had told the maid to get the room ready for Delia, but Morag was there before her, making sure that all her own things were gone before her stepsister arrived. She had not said anything to Pericles and she wilted inwardly when she thought of how he would tease her for taking such a liberty, but he didn't seem to notice at all. In fact he had obviously taken it for granted that she would move into his room as a matter of course. He had said he expected her to sleep in his bed and apparently he thought that was the end of the matter and that she would obey him without any further argument. And she had, though not without a great deal of inner conflict. If he thought it had been easy for her, it hadn't, and one day she would tell him exactly how difficult it had been! Perhaps, one day, she would find the words for that at least!

When the room was ready, she went down to the beach with the children. Kimon could swim quite well, but Peggy was still at the nervous stage when she alternated between wild boasts as to her prowess and shrieks of fear if the water happened to go over her head by accident.

"Will you come in too?" she asked Morag, looking longingly at the bright blue that lapped amiably at her feet.

"Yes. Shall we swim out to that rock?" Morag suggested.

"I can't!" Peggy yelped. "I can't swim as far as that!"

"You said you could yesterday," Kimon reminded her. "Daddy said you couldn't, and you said you could easily!"

"So I can, if Morag comes too!" Peggy claimed, casting a nervous look at the rock in the distance. "She can help me if I get tired."

Kimon squinted a look at Morag. "What are you going to do if Morag needs help too?" he asked, and was off down the beach, feet flying, with Morag in hot pursuit. "You can't catch me!" he jeered over his shoulder.

Morag increased her pace, determined not to be beaten. In doing so, she failed to see Pericles coming towards her, and ran full tilt into him.

"Oh, I'm sorry!" she gasped.

His arms caught her up and swung her round in the air. "Don't be! Shall I catch that young devil for you? What do you want him for?"

"He implied that I couldn't swim out to that rock and back without getting into trouble!"

Pericles looked amused. "Can you? Let's see you do it, then!"

"I'm going to swim there and back too," Peggy said a trifle uncertainly. "Will you watch me too?"

"Okay," said Pericles. "Kimon and I will sit on the beach and laze while you two prove yourselves!" He lowered himself on to the sand and lay back with a self-satisfied air. "Get to it, girls, I shall enjoy watching you!"

Feeling rather foolish, Morag pulled her cap on over her hair and began to walk out the first few feet until she had enough water to swim in. She was very conscious of Pericles making the most of looking her up and down as she took a header into the blue depths and struck out for the black shape of the rock in front of her.

"Wait for me, Morag!" Peggy cried after her.

Morag turned, swimming a few strokes on her back. "Come on, then!"

"I can't go so quickly!" Peggy pushed herself off and began to swim a pedestrian, stately breast-stroke towards Morag. "I'm coming!" she announced triumphantly.

Morag looked over her shoulder at the rock. It served her right, she thought, for wanting to show off to Pericles. She had always been able to swim well and she had wanted to make him admire her for that at least, by flashing through the water out to the rock and back again. But with Peggy slowly coming towards her she had no choice but to slow her strokes to match those of the little girl and to encourage her to do a few more strokes, and then a few more, until at last they reached the rock.

"Do you want to wait a while before we go back?" she asked Peggy.

Peggy nodded, gasping and spluttering as a small wave caught the side of her head. "I don't think I can swim back!"

"Of course you can!"

Peggy clutched at Morag's shoulder, pulling herself closer to the rock. "Daddy will give me a piggy-back if we ask him. He won't mind! He often does it!"

But Morag was determined that they shouldn't have to call upon Pericles. There was no reason, she thought, why she shouldn't give Peggy a lift back to the beach herself. She was strong enough and she could swim as well as anyone she knew.

"You'd better hop on my back," she told Peggy.

The child looked dubiously at her. "You're too small, Morag," she said at last. "I'll push you under. I want Daddy!"

"Of course I'm big enough!" Morag assured her. "I won't let anything happen to you!"

Peggy obediently put her arms round Morag's neck and

sat astride her back, clinging on for dear life. Morag struck out for the shore, using her favourite Australian crawl. But Peggy was far from happy on her precarious perch and tightened her grasp round Morag's neck until she was practically throttling her. Morag put up a hand to release herself and they both rolled over and came up choking.

"You'll drown us both!" Peggy screamed.

"Then don't hold on so tight!"

Peggy began to cry in earnest. "I want Daddy!"

"We'll try again," Morag said patiently. "We haven't far to go now."

"We have! We have!"

"We have not!" Morag snapped. She trod water, allowing herself to look over to where they had left Pericles sitting on the sand, but he was no longer there. For an instant she knew such a sense of desolation that she felt completely ridiculous. He wasn't really gone. He had probably only moved his position – but *where was he*?

"Come on, Peggy, get on my back again!"

Peggy, suddenly silent, did as she was asked. "Daddy's gone," she lamented. "He might have waited!"

Morag thought so too. "Never mind, darling. We can manage quite well without him!"

"We can't!" Peggy said with depressing certainty.

"Of course we can! Do sit still, Peggy! You're throttling me again!"

"I'm trying not to, but I want Daddy! *He* doesn't sink so much when I ride on him!"

Morag forbore to answer. She swam on with a dogged determination, having long since abandoned any attempt at style. All she wanted to do now was arrive without too much damage done to either herself or Peggy.

"I think you could stand on the bottom now," Peggy told her. "I can see the sand through the water."

Morag tried to do as she was told, but the water was deeper than Peggy had supposed and they both submerged

138

and rose again, crosser and more frightened than ever.

"I told you, Morag, I told you! We're going to drown!"

"*No, we are not!*"

She seized the child under her armpits and turning over on to her back began to move with increasing pace towards the shore. Peggy was crying by now and she felt like tears herself. Then, just as she was beginning to give up hope, her shoulders grated against the rough sand and she realised that they were there. She looked up and saw Pericles standing beside her, looking down at her.

"I thought you'd gone!" she accused him.

"I did, but I came back to watch you two nits writhing about in old Poseidon's hair!"

"Don't encourage her," said another, only too familiar voice. "She's hoping you'll give her the kiss of life! Morag can swim like a fish!"

Delia!

Morag leapt to her feet in one swift movement. Her stepsister wore a cool white dress and looked as smart as paint, whereas she, she knew, looked a complete mess, her hair wet and straggly, and the swimming-suit she was wearing so old that she couldn't remember when she had first had it, and without an atom of make-up to hide the freckles that the hot Greek sun had brought out on the bridge of her nose.

"Hullo, Delia," she said in a strained voice.

Delia took a step backwards and looked her up and down, managing to draw attention to the faded colour of the swim-suit and the signs of wear on the straps that would soon fall into holes. "Hullo yourself!" she drawled.

"*Very* cosy!" Delia murmured, looking round the bedroom Morag had helped to prepare for her. "You certainly knew what you were doing when you took off for Greece, didn't you, pet?"

"What do you mean?" Morag countered.

"I should have thought it was obvious. The only flies in the ointment are the children. Is that little girl always such a trial? I'm surprised Pericles allows her to hang round him like that."

"She'd been badly frightened," Morag pointed out. "She wanted to swim out to the rock with me and it was further than she could manage."

"Showing off, I suppose, like you!"

This came uncomfortably close to the truth. "I'm very fond of both the children!" Morag claimed.

"Especially when their father is around? Oh, don't bother to pretend with me! I'd do exactly the same!" Delia sank down on to the bed and looked about her. "Where do you sleep? Or is that one of your little marriage secrets?"

"No." Morag wished that she had outgrown the habit of always having to answer Delia's questions, no matter how inconvenient they were to herself. "I sleep on the other side of the house. Our room looks over the sea too, but it's at the other end."

"*Our* room? Well done, my dear. I thought you were here more or less as governess to those brats." She frowned, her eyes cold and hard. "That's the impression I received from Perry. He isn't in love with you – but I suppose you know that?"

"Did he say so?" Morag couldn't resist asking.

Her stepsister smiled slowly. "Now that would be telling! I must say he's the most attractive man I've seen for a long, long time. He makes David seem a wishy-washy shadow of what a man can be. But then I keep forgetting, you were in love with David, weren't you? Does Pericles know that?"

Morag fiddled with her fingers. "You were in love with David too!"

"Was I?" Delia laughed. Morag remembered that laugh of old. It was supposed to sound like the tinkling of a distant bell and had hours of hard practice behind its

140

soft, clear tones. To Morag it sounded like the knell of doom.

"You said you were. He thought you were too. You know he did! He wouldn't – he wouldn't have taken you out otherwise!"

"Thus dishing you? My dear, I did you a favour. More of a favour than I knew, seeing you might have married him! It would have suited me a great deal better if you had!"

Morag was astonished. "Why?" she asked flatly.

"Why?" Delia laughed again. "Well, really, surely you don't have to ask? It would have suited Pericles a great deal better too!"

Morag made no answer. She pointed out the towels the maid had left beside the dressing-table, and the various other facilities of the room, and then she turned to go. "If there's nothing more you want, I'll be with the children," she said.

Delia yawned delicately. "Oh, but I was hoping you would unpack for me," she smiled. "It was all such a rush, and you know how bad I am at folding things. I'm sure I've forgotten quite half of what I meant to bring with me!"

"Why did you come?" Morag asked.

"Why? I thought you knew. I came to see your husband – at his request – against other things!"

"Then what was all that about your falling out with Daddy?" Morag said bluntly.

"He has been a trifle difficult lately. He was quite reassured when I said you would be home again soon. It was quite touching how worried about you he's been, especially when you think how easily he took the David incident in his stride!"

"Oh?"

"Well, he did think that *you'd* killed David, and I don't suppose he enjoyed the trial and all the gossip. It gave him a shock to find that anything to do with your mother could be less than perfect." She slanted a look of pure dislike at

Morag. "You always were naïve about your father. I suppose you didn't know that he avoided you because you look like your mother? I thought not! What a fool you are, Morag Grant!"

Morag's hands clenched into two fists. "Morag Holmes," she corrected.

Delia got off the bed and went over to the window, looking out at the clear blue sea and the beauty of the headland.

"But not for long," she said to no one in particular. "Not if I can help it!"

CHAPTER TEN

Delia had no hesitation in accepting the offer of the loan of Dora's car. Morag, already on edge by her stepsister's attitude to her mother-in-law, tried in vain to suggest that she should hire her own, or should use the buses as Morag did herself.

"Why should I!?" Delia had asked.

"I should have thought you'd know that!" Morag answered more tartly than she usually spoke to anyone.

But Delia only smiled. "It was you who was banned from driving!"

Morag bit her lip, hoping that Dora hadn't heard that. "I still don't think you ought to take Dora's car. It isn't easy driving in Athens and – and supposing anything should happen?"

"Don't be ridiculous! What should happen? I don't intend to use the car often. Pericles has offered to show me some of the countryside and I'm not likely to turn down an invitation like that to drive myself!"

Morag stiffened. "Where is he taking you?"

"Oh, some place near Athens. Eleusis, or Elefsis, I think he called it. I expect you've already been there?"

"No," said Morag.

"Well, a governess can't expect such little treats, can she? Cheer up, I'll return him to you with a good grace when we get back."

Morag's eyes darkened. "Will you?"

"If he wants to be returned to you. Frankly, my dear, I think he's more likely to have second thoughts about you – like David did! – and make some comparisons between us in which you can hardly expect to show up very well. I

143

nearly died when I saw you in that old swimming-suit! How long have you had it? But then you never did put much value on glamour. David used to say you were the drab sister – "

"I don't believe you!"

"About David? He wasn't the kind, simple young man you thought him at all! I came as quite a relief to him, I can tell you. At least I knew how to kiss and wasn't afraid to have a little fun! Do you bore Pericles too?"

Morag flushed. "I – I don't want to talk about Pericles," she said. "Or David either!"

"No?" Delia was plainly enjoying herself. "You wouldn't! You're the complete coward! Did you tell Pericles that you didn't want me here? Or did you pretend that we'd always loved each other, like good girls should? *He* didn't mind my coming here! I can stay as long as I like!"

Morag said nothing. She looked up as her mother-in-law, until now on the verandah outside, came in and smiled at them both. "Ah, there you are, Delia," she said with every sign of pleasure. "Did Morag tell you that my nephew is staying here for the time being? Pericles is so jealous of Morag that the poor boy has been feeling quite out of things and he'll be all the more pleased to entertain you. I'm expecting him home any time now and I promised him I'd be on hand to introduce you."

Morag stared at her mother-in-law in astonishment, only to receive a fierce dig in the ribs and a command in Greek to sit up and behave herself, which she recognised as much by the tone of voice as by how often she had heard the same rebuke addressed to Peggy.

"Pericles has asked Delia to visit Eleusis," Morag said in a small voice.

Dora sniffed. "A very industrial site," she commented. "I suppose he wants the children to see it. They are beginning to interest themselves in growing things and it's time they learned the story of Demeter and how she gave the

144

first crops to humanity. Of course she was worshipped there more as the mother of Persephone, who came back from the dead. But I don't suppose you want to hear our old stories, do you? You look a very modern young lady to me."

It was obvious that Delia wasn't sure whether this was a compliment or not. "I like to enjoy myself," she said, less sure of herself than Morag had ever seen her.

"With my son?" Dora looked faintly bored. "He looks more Greek than English, don't you think?" Her eyes narrowed. "Do his looks please you?".

"Why yes, I suppose so," Delia answered.

"In Greece, it is the woman who pleases the man!"

Delia managed a light laugh. "Isn't that kind of thing reciprocal anywhere?"

"Do you think so?" Dora, too, laughed softly. "No, a man may play with a pretty toy, but when it comes to his wife – then he will make sure that he is the only man in her life. Marriage, in Greece, is not a thing to be taken lightly. Every Greek wants a bride who will put him at the centre of her existence. Morag makes the ideal wife for Pericles in that respect."

Delia opened her eyes very wide, looking the picture of innocence. "But didn't you know? Morag was engaged to another man before she came to Greece!"

Dora looked at her with dry amusement. "You mean this David of yours? If Morag had been a Greek girl, she would have been protected from the attentions of a man like that! Girls of good family are not made use of by their relations in that way here, not even by their more worldly-wise sisters!"

"Ouch!" said Delia. "Some time I'll tell you my side of that story, Mrs. Holmes. Morag isn't always very reliable when it comes to telling the truth!"

"Morag has yet to tell me anything." Dora rose to her feet. "She didn't have to. I know very little about her family, as a matter of fact, but she has a family here now

145

and she is very dear to us all." She made a more familiar gesture of impatience. "Those children! For heaven's sake, Morag, go and see to them! I will not have them making such a noise in the house. It's time Peggy learned a little restraint and didn't shriek like that!"

Morag needed no second bidding. She much preferred the company of the children just now. They knew nothing of the undercurrents Delia had brought with her, that swirled dangerously about Morag, threatening her happiness with the spite of years. It was good of Dora to defend her as she had, but it was Pericles' opinion that mattered, and Pericles had agreed to Delia coming to Greece. Worse still, he showed every sign of enjoying her company as much as David had before him!

Morag did her best not to encourage the children when they told her what they thought of her stepsister.

"She's awful!" Kimon said stolidly.

"Yes," said Peggy, "she's awful!"

"But she's very pretty," Morag said.

"I like looking at you better," Peggy assured her. "I don't want to draw *her*. Her eyes are awful! You have nice green eyes, hers aren't even blue! They're – " She broke off at a loss for words. "They're horrid!"

Kimon nodded. "Like pebbles," he put in.

"Some people think pebbles very pretty," Morag said, trying not to laugh. "Her eyes are grey, if you want to know!"

"They're not. They're not anything much – *and* she changed into a blue dress and they still weren't anything much!"

Morag gave Peggy an exasperated look. "Don't let her hear you say that!"

"Why not?" Kimon asked. "If Peggy were to paint her, she would have to know, wouldn't she? It seems a reasonable thing to discuss to me."

"Oh, does it? Well, I think it's just an excuse for making

146

personal remarks! She's my stepsister, don't forget!"

"But you don't like her either," Peggy stated as a known fact.

"Do you?" Kimon added, his smile the image of his father's when he was most determined to bend her to his will. "You said you thought her silly, and so she is! You should have seen her when she arrived, running down the steps to the beach and practically sitting on top of Daddy! I hope she knows that he married you?" he added, giving the coin he was looking at a fierce jab with his finger. "You did tell her, didn't you?"

"Of course she knows!" Morag replied. "She was there when we got married."

"Oh, good!" the boy said with relief. "She can have Takis if she likes."

Peggy nodded soberly. "Good idea," she agreed.

"No, it isn't a good idea. It's a terrible idea, unless they both happen to want it that way," Morag protested. "Why were you making so much noise just now? Grandma doesn't like it when you shout at one another in the house!" It was bad enough that Dora should have decided that Takis could entertain Delia, without the children getting the same idea! No, Morag wanted her stepsister gone as quickly as possible, not playing around with anyone as close to the family as Takis.

"We were having an argument," Kimon told her.

"About you," Peggy added.

"Me?" Morag asked.

Kimon turned and looked at her. "Did you invite Delia here, or did she ask herself? Peggy says that Daddy asked her!"

Morag replied abruptly. "She asked herself!" she said.

"That's what I thought," said Kimon. "But Peggy says she heard Daddy and Grandma talking, and that Daddy said – "

"I don't want to know!"

147

"He said you'd never be free," Peggy went on where her brother had left off, "not until she came. Grandma said it was an awful risk!"

"You shouldn't repeat other people's conversations," Morag quelled her. What had Pericles meant – she would never be free? She felt weak at the knees and more vulnerable than ever. Could he have meant free of him?

The children stared at her. "Are you all right, Morag?" Peggy asked.

"Yes, I'm all right. Will you be quiet now if I go and change for dinner?"

"Of course!" they agreed, full of injured innocence. "What are you going to wear?" Peggy said almost in the same breath. "I suppose your gold dress would be too grand?"

"Yes, I think so," Morag said, not thinking what she was saying. "I'm going to wear my jade pendant, though."

Peggy screwed up her face thoughtfully. "Yes," she approved. "And with your hair loose. Daddy likes it better that way."

Now when could she have heard him say that? Morag wondered. Had he really voiced an opinion and, if he had, what else had he said?

It seemed strange not to go to the room she had had before, the one which was now Delia's. She had to restrain herself from knocking on the door of Perry's room. It didn't seem like hers at all. To her relief it was empty. She turned on the light feeling like a burglar. She was glad to see that there was no trace of her possessions anywhere. At least she didn't have to feel she was imposing on him.

The dress she chose to wear was not new. Delia would have seen it hundreds of times before, she thought with a wry smile in the glass, but she looked nice in it and part of the pattern was green to match the jade pendant Pericles had given her. It made her eyes look greener than ever too, and she thought how suitable that was too. Green-eyed meant jealous, and that was exactly what she was. She was jealous of any other woman Pericles looked at.

She brushed her hair into a cloud round her head, ready to fasten it into the nape of her neck. Then she hesitated. Should she leave it free as Kimon had suggested? She fingered the loose ends and decided that she would, even if it did make her look younger and as vulnerable as she felt. Last of all, she looked for the jade pendant to hang round her neck, but she couldn't find it anywhere. Annoyed to think that she had left it behind when she had brought the rest of her things from the other room, she decided she would have to go back to Delia's room to look for it. She hurried down the corridor before she could change her mind, coming to a stop outside the door.

At first she sould not believe her ears. It was Pericles that she could hear through the shut door. She stood completely still, unable to bring herself to move, just as Delia's tinkling bell laugh rang out. A second later the door opened and Pericles stood before her.

"What do you want?" he asked her.

"I – " She put a hand up to her mouth, found herself quite unable to continue, and turned on her heel and fled.

She did not get far. His arm flashed out and held her hard against him. "Well, Morag? Are you reducing to listening outside doors now?"

"No," she whispered.

"No? Then what are you doing?"

It was ridiculous to feel so guilty. Surely it was he who was that! What had he been doing in Delia's room?

He let her go with a suddenness that unbalanced her and had to put out a hand against the wall to save herself from falling. "Well, I hope you liked what you heard!" Pericles shot at her.

"I didn't hear anything!"

"Then what were you doing?"

She tried to hide her face from him. "I wanted my jade
149

pendant. I must have left it behind when I moved – moved my things – "

"Into my room?"

She nodded, rubbing her shoulder where she had caught it against the wall. "May I get past, please?"

There was an inscrutable look on his face. "I didn't know you'd moved," he told her. "I couldn't see any of your things around. Do you always keep everything so neat?"

"Please, may I get past?"

His eyes glinted. "What will you give me if I do?"

"*Nothing*." She was very sure of that. She gave a mutinous lift to her chin. "I wonder you should ask since you've probably already had everything you can want from Delia!"

His hand caught her round the arm and hauled her relentlessly back into the room she now shared with him. With his other hand, he slammed the door shut behind them.

"Now," he said, "you can tell me exactly what you mean by that!"

She licked her lips nervously. "I only meant – "

"Yes?"

"Nothing," she said.

"That won't do, Morag. For once you're going to tell me just what's going on inside that head of yours. What should I want from Delia?"

She struggled vainly against his restricting hands. "She's – very attractive!" she said feebly.

"Yes, she is," he agreed readily.

The colour came and went in her cheeks. Her eyes fell before his. "I know you find her attractive."

"And you're jealous of her? Is that what you're trying to say?"

"No, of course not! I think she's attractive too!"

"Is that so?" he drawled. "It seems to me that you don't like her at all. Why don't you ask outright what I was doing in her room?"

"Oh!" she gasped. "You can do as you like!"

"I shall," he retorted.

She wept inwardly. As if she didn't know that! The first time he had seen Delia, he had wanted to kiss her – he had even asked Morag if she thought he could as her future stepbrother-in-law. And it hadn't stopped there! He had insisted that she came to Greece for as long as she wanted, regardless of anything that Morag had said to him. And now he was visiting her in her room!

"You promised that you would pretend to my family that you – that you *liked* me!" she reminded him on a note of desperation.

"I promised I'd protect your pride *while we were in England*. But, if you remember, I told you the price you'd have to pay for my pride would ask a great deal more than a few kisses of you!"

"I – I didn't agree to pay any price for your pride!" she stammered.

"You haven't any choice – as my wife," he pointed out.

She wrenched herself away from him. "I've done everything you asked! I don't see what more I can do!"

He looked at her thoughtfully. "I can't remember that you've actually offered anything," he said. "If it had been left to you, you'd still be addressing me as Mr. Holmes!"

"Oh," her stifled gasp betrayed her consternation. "But I told you that – that I liked – " her voice dropped to a whisper, "you to kiss me"

"I might like being kissed by you!"

She was silent for so long that she thought he'd lose all patience with her, but he went on standing there, waiting, "Delia would like to kiss you," she said.

His mouth kicked up at the corners. "You don't say!"

Her eyes flew to his face. "You mean you knew why she came here?"

"I'd be a fool not to, my dear, I have a certain amount of experience of your sex, I am not in the least bit sorry to say. If she succeeds, though, you will have only yourself to blame."

She gave him a look of mute enquiry. If he could read Delia with such ease, could he also read the secrets of her heart? she wondered.

"You could compete with her," he told her dryly. "I find you attractive too, as you very well know!"

Her heart jerked within her. "But I'm your wife!" she exclaimed.

He nodded soberly at her. "Yes, you are. Don't let me have to remind you of it again!"

He stood back and opened the door for her, a glint of amusement in his eyes. She couldn't bring herself to look up at him, but took to her heels and fled down the corridor, anywhere, just so that she could be out of sight of his mocking challenge.

Delia's triumphant air was very hard to bear. Morag watched her covertly across the table and was astonished at the depth of feeling that consumed her whenever her stepsister's tinkling laughter rang out in response to some sally from Pericles. Delia knew exactly what she was doing. It was the old, old story, unfolding like a tired, seen-too-often-film, of finding someone else's grass much greener than one's own. Morag had watched it all before, only then it had been David whom Delia had wanted and Morag had been able to find all sorts of excuses for her, and for David too, who had fallen flat at Delia's feet and had taken it for granted that Morag would understand.

She had understood, that was the trouble. Naturally, David had found Delia more interesting and more fun than herself, everybody always did. It had been just the same at school where Morag had once heard one of Delia's friends commiserating her for having to live with such a dull person.

"Morag never says anything," the girl had complained.

152

"How do you live with her silent criticism of you all the time?"

Delia had laughed. At the time she had still been practising the tinkling bell laugh and it hadn't always worked. That time it had slipped into an off-key bray. "Nobody likes Morag," she had said.

It wasn't true, of course. There had been many people who had liked Morag very much, many who had preferred her vastly to her stepsister, but they had never been made welcome at the Grant house and Morag had practically given up asking them to her home. But such remarks don't have to be true to be hurtful, and it had been one of a whole series of pinpricks that had robbed her of much of her confidence, more especially when she came into contact with anyone new who had not known her since her babyhood, when her mother had been alive and had surrounded her with all the love she needed.

David had liked her at first. He had broken into her thirst for friendship like a glass of cool, clear water. He had particularly liked to dance with her. "You should always be seen when you're doing something," he had told her. "Never sitting still!" She hadn't paid him much attention, but she had been pleased that he had thought about her at all.

After a while, she had even taken him home. It had been a curious, platonic relationship, with David making use of her notes and very often asking her to write his essays as well as her own for the tutor they shared at the college they both attended. "When we've done with all these exams," he'd said to her one day, "I'll put you out to work and let you keep me for ever!"

It had seemed to Morag the most glorious moment of her life. "Do you mean you'll marry me?" she had asked him.

He had shrugged his shoulders, as shy as she. "Why not?" he had said.

It was only then that Delia had started taking an interest in him. In a moment of weakness when Delia had been

153

feeling particularly charming, Morag had confided in her that she and David were getting married. "Not yet!" she had said, "but one day when David has a proper job." She had forgotten all about his threat to send her out to work for him!

Delia had smiled at David and then she laughed. "A man," she had said, with a flutter of her eyelashes, "would want more than the cool embrace of someone as innocent as Morag Grant. It takes an old man to want liking instead of love – a young man should be looking for fire and enthusiasm, something that Morag could never rise to!"

David had promptly thought so too. He had tried to explain to Morag the excitement he found in being with her stepsister, when Morag had found the two of them entwined on the sofa in her father's study one Sunday afternoon. "One has to have a bit of fun!" he had ended, looking considerably ill at ease.

Well, they'd had their fun and Morag tried not to mind. Once or twice she had tried to clear up her own position as far as David was concerned, but he had put her off with the occasional date, telling her that she didn't understand. Delia didn't mean anything to him! But that, she had thought, was a lie, for he had gone on seeing far more of Delia than he ever had of herself, right up until that last, terrible night when she had crashed the car and killed him.

"David always said you'd do anything he asked you to!" Delia had sobbed. She had looked remarkably unattractive at that moment, her face grey with shock, and her clothes and hair mussed as much from David's attentions as from the crash.

"You'd better get into bed," Morag had said. "I'll go down to the car and wait for the police."

It had been better that way. It had been the way David would have wanted it. But Delia could not have Pericles too! Morag sat back in her chair and looked at her stepsister with a cold, objective eye. She was attractive, of course, but it was a shop-worn, Christmas decoration kind of attraction that looked tawdry in the full light of day. Little hard lines were beginning to crease her face from nose to mouth and, though she laughed frequently, her eyes were hard and never laughed at all. Morag had always known her to be selfish, but it had not previously occurred to her that Delia never gave anything away. She would take from any man, but she would give nothing that was worthwhile in return.

Morag stared at her as though she had never seen her before, and, in a way, she hadn't. She had always thought of Delia as being beautiful and easy to love, but she wasn't. She was merely brittle and grasping and – and rather tedious! How odd, Morag thought, to find out now that Delia was scarcely worth the trouble of disliking, for she wasn't anything very much.

She most certainly wasn't good enough for Pericles!

"I'm sorry, what did you say?" Morag turned to her mother-in-law as though she were emerging from a dream. "I – I wasn't listening!"

"That, my dear, was quite obvious!" Dora rasped her. "You ought to have something better to do than day-dreaming at the dinner table! As Pericles' wife you have a duty to help entertain your guests! Takis is still waiting to be introduced to your sister!"

Morag gave a little shrug of her shoulders. "I'm sorry," she said again.

Dora shook herself irritably. "In Greece we prize hospitality very highly. You must learn to be a better hostess than that! My husband would have had something to say to me if I hadn't waited on his guests with my own hands! Pericles is too soft with you!"

Morag was not as afraid of her mother-in-law as she had been at one time. She smiled, tongue in cheek, "But you are still the hostess here!"

Dora picked up her knife and rapped her smartly over

155

the knuckles. In this mood, it was easy to see why Peggy sometimes disliked her. "This house belongs to Pericles, not to me – "

Pericles leaned across the table and took the knife from his mother. "Leave Morag alone, Mama," he said. He smiled straight at Morag, with such a look that her breath was taken away. "If anyone beats her, I shall!" he added. The glint in his eyes grew more pronounced. "I see you found your pendant," he added.

"Morag never took care of anything," Delia put in. "She would have turned my whole room upside down if I hadn't found it for her. My mother would never allow her to have anything of value in case she lost it. If she didn't lose it, she'd give it away! David said she'd have given away her engagement ring if he'd given her one!"

"Would you give away my ring?" Pericles asked Morag. She fingered her wedding ring and shook her head. "Of course not!"

"She'll probably lose it!" Delia sighed.

"If she does I'll definitely beat her," Pericles drawled. His eyes lingered on Morag's hot face with a faint smile, then he turned away from her and gave all his attention to Delia, drawing her out with a charm that made her seem suddenly nicer and added a sparkle to her replies.

"I hope you haven't forgotten that I'm taking you to Eleusis tomorrow," he reminded her. "You'll have to ask Morag to tell you about the place, if you don't already know about it. She has all the old legends at her fingertips – an interest she shares with my mother."

"Are you taking the children?" Dora asked, obviously still annoyed at the way Pericles had taken her knife from her.

"I don't think so," Pericles answered.

"It's good for them to see these places!" their grand-mother declared. "You needn't think I'm going to look after them all day tomorrow, because I'm painting in the

156

morning and playing bridge in the afternoon."

"Morag will look after them," Pericles said smoothly.

Morag looked up quickly. "But I'd like to come," she protested. "They say it isn't much to look at now, but it must have had terrific atmosphere at one time. The rites of Demeter and Persephone meant everything to such a lot of people. Persephone was the first one to come back from the dead, even in legend, as an ordinary person!"

"You can see it some other time," Pericles told her. "It will be too long a day for the children, and anyway, I want some time with Delia by herself."

Morag blinked. "The children will be disappointed – "

Pericles threw back his head in an arrogant gesture. "But neither they nor you have been invited to come with us tomorrow. They won't be disappointed if you don't tell them about it."

But she did know, Morag thought resentfully. He might have married her to look after the children, but he didn't have to fling it in her face in front of Delia. And she was more than ever determined that Delia would have to go, and go quickly. The only thing she didn't know was how she was going to get rid of her.

CHAPTER ELEVEN

MORAG went to bed before her husband. She heard him come in almost an hour later and pretended to be asleep. When he turned on the light she almost gave herself away, flinching away from the sudden glare in her eyes. Her heart pounded, for she was almost sure that he wouldn't spare her feelings if he were to guess she was awake. When he came over to the bed she held her breath. He stood for a long time, looking down at her, but he said nothing. He bent down and pushed a lock of her hair away from her mouth with gentle fingers. Almost then she gave way to the urgent desire within her to open her arms to him and to whisper her love for him, but the thought of how he had snubbed her when she had asked him if she, too, could go to Eleusis restrained her. Yet she might have changed her mind if he had touched her again, but he did not. He turned out the light and lay down on the bed beside her, pulling her into the hard circle of his arm. He must have known then that she was awake, but he still said nothing, and he was asleep long before she could still the loud beating of her heart and relax against him sufficiently to fall into slumber herself.

Her dreams when they came were muddled and confused. Dora had made her tell her stepsister the story of Demeter's long search for her daughter, and how she had served the royal family at Eleusis as nursemaid to their child and, becoming fond of the child, had decided to make him immortal by toughening him in the flames. Not surprisingly, the queen had thought she had intended to burn the child to death, and Demeter had been forced to reveal herself as a goddess. In return for the royal family's kindness, she has made Eleusis the centre of her worship. It was there too that Persephone came back from the kingdom of the dead, no longer a goddess because she had eaten the seeds of the pomegranate during her time under the earth and she was now fated to spend four months of the year with her husband, Hades, and the remaining eight in the service of her mother. Hence her new name of Kore, or Maiden, in token of her new position in the first sacred family of Greece. Morag had once seen a statue of Demeter, her arms outstretched, her face grieving for her loss, and she saw the heavy stone figure again in her dream and she knew exactly who she was, but the other figure, also a woman, came right up to her, a look of vengeance in her eyes, but when she saw the necklace of shells around Morag's neck she faded away again, changing her shape into that of a man, a man Morag recognised as Pericles, though it didn't really look much like him.

"Who are you?" she cried out.

"Hush, who do you think I am? I'm Pericles!"

It was Pericles all right, but she didn't know if she were waking or sleeping. "It was Nemesis," she said firmly.

"How do you know that?"

"She recognised my shell necklace."

"I think, my dear, that you have been dreaming."

"I suppose so, because she turned into you!"

"Into me?" He pulled her close and kissed her. "I hope that gave you joy!"

She hid her face against him. "Yes, it did," she said. "I'm sorry I woke you, Perry."

He pulled her closer still. "I'm not," he said.

In the morning her dream seemed very far away. Delia, on the other hand, was a very present reality. Morag saw her coming down the path to the beach, a little unsure in her fashionable platform shoes.

"I hope you aren't allowing that silly child out of her

depth today?" Delia panted. She looked very pleased with herself and Morag thought she knew why.

"Have you come down to swim?" she returned.

"Dressed like this? Really, I don't know how you can be so stupid! I'm waiting for Pericles!"

"Oh yes?"

Delia almost laughed out loud. "Poor Morag, but you didn't think he was in love with you, did you? You weren't as stupid as that? That was quite a snub he gave you yesterday, but you never learn! You ought to know by now why he wants to be alone with me!"

Morag kept her temper with difficulty. "Should I?"

"What have you to offer a man like Pericles? I can't think how you persuaded him to marry you."

Morag wasn't sure either, but she had no intention of sharing her doubts with her stepsister. "I don't suppose you can," she said quietly.

"I thought you might have flattered him into it, but, knowing you, you probably haven't told him that you've fallen in love with him. He's very Greek, isn't he? Having a name like that would be ridiculous for most men, but it suits him in an extraordinary way. I suppose that's why he took you on. He can't have found it very lively living with his mother in semi-exile here. Anything would be better than nothing under the circumstances!"

Morag gave her a mocking look. "It's hard to tell!"

Delia frowned, for once uncertain how to deal with her stepsister. "Any man will take what's offered to him!"

"You should know!"

Delia's cold eyes glazed with anger. "You'll regret that! You're a fool, Morag! I hold your happiness in the hollow of my hand. You didn't mind when I took David, did you? But Pericles? You won't like losing him to me!"

"Pericles goes his own way!"

"My way," Delia rejoined. She stared long and hard at Morag. "Why, I believe you're even afraid of him!" she laughed, and there was very little of the tinkling bell about it. "So I'll be doing you a favour by taking him from you!"

"But why?" Morag asked. "Why do you want to hurt me?"

Delia turned away, putting one foot on a loose stone that slipped underneath her. If Morag had not held her upright, she would have fallen. "Don't you know why?" she said in a low and deadly voice. "I hate you, Morag Grant. I hate you for always being right and for doing all the right things! If I took your favourite toy, you'd offer me your next favourite after I'd broken it for you! The less you had, the less you needed. Even David – you couldn't be content with handing me him on a plate, but you had to sacrifice yourself to his memory and my good name. Who asked you to? Who asked you?"

"But I thought you wanted me to!"

"Well, you shouldn't think!" Delia pulled away from Morag, examining her shoes. "Why are you afraid of Pericles?"

"I'm not."

"But you said you were!"

"If you say so –" Morag's face was controlled.

"Well, there you are, then! What's the difference? I'll bet he knows it too and thinks he can treat you how he likes! I wouldn't put up with it! In fact I shall quite enjoy teaching him a lesson. Of course, he's madly attractive too. I like a man who doesn't mind taking the initiative. And I don't think there's any danger of his *not* liking me, do you?"

Morag stopped herself from giving Delia a shove that would have sent her flying on those ridiculous shoes. That, she told herself, was not the way to deal with her. There had to be a better more civilised way, if only she could think of it! "Pericles is a married man," she said, seething inwardly, because if that was the best argument she could find, she might just as well hand him over on a plate to Delia here and now.

161

"Oh, hardly, darling!" Delia's laugh was well in control now and sounded more bell-like than ever. "I don't suppose you'd have put so much as a foot in his room if I hadn't happened to be coming! It's obvious that he doesn't think of you in that way at all!"

Morag clenched her fists. "Why do you say that?" she asked quietly. A fine thing it would be if she were to burst into tears now and give Delia such an easy victory!

Delia smiled, savouring the moment. "Well, dear, David always said that you were too nice to be much of a temptation, and, if you're very inexperienced, it's so easy to mistake good manners for anything warmer. I'm sure Pericles has lovely manners!"

"I don't see how you could know that," Morag protested.

The laugh came again. "Pericles and I had a lovely long talk together last night. I don't intend to waste my time while I'm here!"

Morag was scarcely aware of the cries of the children as they chased each other along the length of the beach. She watched them for a long pregnant moment, but she didn't see them at all. She took a deep breath. "I think it would be better if you went back to England, Delia," she said at last.

"I'm sure you do, sweetie, but I'm having too nice a time here. Life has been frightfully dull since David died – and he was rather dull too, or he would have been if he hadn't got involved with you."

"I don't think you understand me," Morag went on quietly. "I'm telling you to go. I'll see about your ticket myself, and my mother-in-law will drive you to the airport."

Delia's laugh was not quite so well under control this time. "And what will Pericles say to that?" Delia demanded. "He'll take my side! You know he will, just as he did last night!"

"My husband won't know until you've gone."

"Your husband? My God, that's rich! Don't you think

162

that I might tell him? It was he who invited me here –"

"Did he?" Morag asked coolly.

Delia's eyelashes flickered. "I wrote to him in the first place, but he wrote straight back and told me to come!"

"And now I'm telling you to go!"

Delia sat down hard, almost as though her knees had given way underneath her. Morag regarded her cautiously. It would be a mistake to think that after all these years Delia could be as easy to deal with as that.

"Aren't you afraid what Pericles will do to you?" Delia demanded.

She was, but there was no need to dwell on that, Morag told herself. "Perry won't hurt me," she said.

"He might, if that old woman is to be believed. She goes on as if Greek husbands were little tin gods and do exactly as they like to their wives!"

Morag smiled slowly. "Well, I don't see myself making Perry do anything he doesn't want to do, can you? Why should I? I like it very well that he's the boss and holds the reins, but he wouldn't hurt me. He's too big a person for that."

Delia gave her a condescending look. "You never knew anything about David. What makes you think you can read Pericles any better?"

"I wasn't married to David," Morag answered with a calmness she was far from feeling. "Shall I help you pack?"

But Delia ignored the question. "What will you tell him? I mean about my not going to Eleusis with him?"

"I don't know," Morag admitted. "I may talk him into taking the children and me after all."

Delia narrowed her cold eyes; she flicked a lock of fair hair out of her eyes and then pulled on it thoughtfully. "You haven't got rid of me yet. Really, Morag, I don't see how you're going to. You can hardly put me physically out of the house – I might fight back!"

Morag straightened her back, squaring her shoulders.

"I'll ask Dora to drive us both to the airport," she began.

"And what about the children?"

Morag had forgotten all about her charges. What was she going to do with them? "They're not babies," she said aloud. "Peggy has a whole lot more stamps to stick in, and Kimon can always find something to do."

"Let's hope Pericles will agree with you!" The laugh rang out again, and Morag was very conscious of the new note of confidence in Delia's voice. "You're storing up a terrible bust-up for yourself with that so-called husband of yours! I think I'll stick around and see the fun. I came here to teach you a lesson, but I shan't have to lift a finger to do anything after all. You'll do it all yourself! Go ahead, Morag, it'll do you more harm than good!"

Repelled by the dislike in Delia's face, Morag clenched her fists. "I will!" she said wildly. "I'll get rid of you if it's the last thing I do!"

"It'll be the last thing you do as Mrs. Pericles Holmes!" Delia retorted.

Morag felt cold despite the hot sun beating down on her. "We'll see," she said grimly.

She turned on her heel and walked up the path towards the house, resisting the temptation to take the steps two at a time just in case she fell flat on her face, for she had no intention of granting Delia the satisfaction of such a spectacle. There was no sound of movement in the house. At least that was one problem out of the way, for to have run into Pericles at that moment would have destroyed the last vestiges of the courage that she had fought with herself for so long to bring to a steaming head. She had to make Delia go – there could be no turning back on that. If Pericles wanted her, it was too bad!

Morag wouldn't give herself time to change her mind. If she didn't do it now, in the heat of the moment, she knew herself well enough to know that she would never do it at all, and then she would deserve to lose Pericles.

But Delia should not have him! No matter what Pericles had to say to her, Morag couldn't allow that. She was his wife and, even if he couldn't love her, she would try to be content with what he could give her. Indeed, she couldn't imagine how she could live without him now that he had taught her what it meant to love a man so much that all else paled into insignificance beside the wonder of it.

She swept into Delia's room and began to shove her clothing into her open suitcase. It was like her stepsister not to have found the time to unpack, not even her evening dresses, nor her sponge-bag, but then perhaps she hadn't felt the need to wash since her arrival the day before. It helped to stoke the fires of Morag's rage and she seized on it with relief. She banged the suitcase shut and dumped it down on the floor, pushing it across the floor. As she pulled open the door, she was confronted by her astonished mother-in-law.

"What *are* you doing?" Dora demanded. She had a paintbrush in her hand and was plainly cross at having been disturbed in her work.

"Packing," Morag answered briefly.

"I can see that. But can't Delia do her own packing?"

Morag wrinkled up her nose. "No." She sat down on the bed, trying to regain the pure flame of her anger. "I've told Delia she must go."

Dora started. "You haven't! What did Pericles say?"

"He doesn't know yet."

"Oh! Oh, Morag, do you think that was a good idea?"

Morag nodded. "I told her you'd drive her to the airport. Will you, Dora? I'll make it all right with Pericles. I'd drive her myself, only you know I can't."

"Yes, but, my dear, if she won't go, what will you do then?"

"She has to go!"

Dora sat down on the bed beside her. "Has she made you very unhappy?"

165

Morag nodded again. "She wants Pericles!"

"She may well, but does Pericles want her?" Dora waved her paintbrush in the air, uttering a small sound of annoyance as some of the paint fell on the blanket. "I think you're making too much of this. The Greeks have a deep respect for the institution of marriage, and Pericles is entirely Greek in that respect. Believe me, if he hadn't, his marriage to Susan would have foundered long before her death."

"She hates me," Morag said simply.

Dora bridled, spattering yet more paint on the bed-clothes. "Oh, my dear!" she murmured. "Are you sure?"

"I think she always has, only I didn't know it. I never guessed that it was that that lay between us. I can't think why she should have thought that I was any kind of a threat to her, but it seems she did. Yet I always gave way to her in everything –"

"But after all these years of putting up with her, why has she suddenly got to go?"

"She says she's come to take Pericles away from me."

"She *said* so?"

"I've never given her any reason to think I'll fight back, only –"

"Only this time you will?"

"This time I'm fighting for my life. I can't let her have Pericles even – even if he wants to go. Will you help me, Dora?"

"Shouldn't you be asking Pericles to do that?"

"Oh no!" Morag shook her head vigorously. "I must do it all myself. You see, I haven't told him – I mean, I don't want him to know –"

"Pericles has a right to know!"

Morag swallowed. "I'll tell him afterwards. If he's angry with anyone, he'll be angry with me!"

"But he did say –"

"I don't care what he said! Delia is going. I'll have it out with Pericles afterwards!"

Dora looked less convinced than ever. "He's fond of you, Morag, or he wouldn't have stopped me yesterday – *I* would never have been allowed to speak to *my* mother-in-law like that! – but it will be a different story if he finds you have defied him. His indulgence with your English ways will stop short at that!"

Morag found herself grinning. "I'll try to be very Greek – afterwards!" she promised. "Perry will probably see to that!"

"I certainly hope so!" her mother-in-law retorted. "Has she got an air ticket back to England?"

"She hasn't got a reservation yet," Morag answered. "That's another thing I want you to do – telephone the airport and get her a seat on the plane."

"But what are you going to do for money?" Dora protested.

Morag's grin grew broader. "Take it out of the housekeeping!"

There was still no sign of Pericles anywhere. Morag took a look outside and was surprised to see that his car had gone as well.

"Where did Daddy go?" she asked Kimon who was coming running up the path from the beach. "Delia didn't go with him, did she?"

Kimon shook his head. "I'm afraid Delia got a little wet," he said in innocent tones. "Peggy and I thought we'd show her some of the jellyfish that the Greek children next door had fished out of the sea. She fell in!"

Morag hardly took in this information. "Did you see Daddy?"

"Yes, of course. We told him Delia didn't want to go with him. Was that right?" Morag looked at him quickly. Surely the children wouldn't have deliberately –? If they had, she thought, it was very much better that she didn't know anything about it.

"Where's Delia now?" she asked.

167

"Down there," he jerked his head back down the path. "Peggy's helping her. She's all right, Morag."

Delia, however, thought she was far from all right as she came up the path a few seconds later. "Look what those brats did to me!" she shouted angrily. "Where's Pericles? I'm going to tell him how you've all treated me."

"I'm afraid Pericles has already left," Morag smiled. "I'm so sorry."

"Are you?" Delia took a step towards Morag and slapped her across the face. "All right, I'll go! But you haven't heard the last of this, Morag Grant. I'll finish you with Pericles, and I'll finish you at home too!"

Morag was aware only of the expression on the children's faces. "It's all right," she reassured them. "She won't really hurt me. She's just a bit cross."

"She's silly," Kimon opined. "Silly and beastly!"

"And you're a horrid little boy!" Delia snapped back. "Look at me! Just look at me! They deliberately drenched me – they knew I was scared of those jellyfish! They were huge and – and ugly!" She turned on Morag. "Don't pretend you're sorry, because I won't believe you! You may have used those brats to get me out of the house, but I don't give up so easily! I'll write to Pericles and tell him how you've all treated me –"

"Daddy will be glad!" Peggy interrupted her. "He doesn't like you either!"

"Peggy!" Her grandmother's tone froze them all to the spot. "Peggy, you will apologise at one. It will be I who will be speaking to Pericles about this. I will not countenance such a disgraceful lapse in good manners in any grand-daughter of mine!"

"I'm sorry, Grandma."

"It is Delia who will have to excuse you, not me, child!"

Peggy flashed a rebellious glance in Delia's direction. "I won't!" she declared. "*She* slapped Morag, and I'm not a bit sorry!"

168

Dora's look of distaste would have turned Morag's bones to jelly, but Delia was made of sterner stuff. "Sisters can be expected to have their quarrels," she said casually. "Morag and I always have had our differences."

"How fortunate that you didn't both turn out badly," Dora murmured with deadly charm. "My daughter-in-law has asked me to take you to the airport, Miss – I'm so sorry, I don't believe I know your name?"

"Miss Price," Delia supplied.

"Well, Miss Price, I have booked and paid for your seat on the next plane back to London myself. So, if you are ready to leave –"

"Like this? I shall have to change!" Delia flung a vindictive look in Morag's direction. "Morag, I can't go like this!"

Morag's face was expressionless. "I'll help you change," she offered. She picked up Delia's suitcase and carried it back into the house with Delia teetering along beside her, her high platform soles slipping out of control on the highly polished marble floor.

"You'll be sorry that you weren't nicer to me!" she threatened. "I shall tell your father –"

"Tell him anything you please."

"Don't you care?" At another time Delia's bewilderment would have made Morag laugh. How odd, she thought, that this time she didn't care what Delia did! If her father didn't know them both by this time he never would, and she didn't think he would judge her too harshly. After all these years, Delia's threatened tale-telling had lost its venom.

Delia saw that she had failed. "What are you going to tell Pericles? *He* won't appreciate having his guests bundled on to the first plane out of the country!"

"I don't know." Morag's tone was even.

"I suppose that mother-in-law of yours will tell him some story to save your bacon! I thought at first she didn't like you – it was all right when *she* hit you, I noticed! – and yet she protects you. I wonder why?"

Morag was silent for a moment. "She has her reasons," she said then.

Delia looked up from putting on a clean pair of tights. "Oh? What?"

But Morag wasn't prepared to tell her. It was enough that she herself should know that Dora tolerated her simply because she worshipped the ground that Pericles walked on. Her stepsister would not view such a weakness with kind eyes. To her, love had always been a matter of taking, just as Morag thought it meant giving and no more than that. She knew better now! Pericles had taught her that! Love meant loving and being loved, and one had to have both elements for it to be perfect.

The children were openly jubilant over Delia's temperature.

Morag at first flushed with triumph, then began to worry. She felt depressed and shaky and very close to tears.

"What do you want to do this afternoon?" she asked the children.

They shrugged their shoulders. "Don't care," Peggy said. "Grandma said she might take us out somewhere."

"But Grandma is playing bridge," Morag reminded them.

Kimon's eyes lit, and he smiled the tantalising smile that was so like his father's. "I think she's put it off," he said.

Dora, when she came back, took one look at Morag's face and told her with some asperity to pull herself together. "My dear girl, Delia's your stepsister. If you wanted her to go, you had a perfect right to get rid of her."

"Even against Pericles' wishes?"

Dora looked considerably less certain. "Well, I expect you'll be able to explain it to him," she said bravely. "But it's no good looking like a guilty shadow! What you need is a little time to yourself to put some spirit back into you –"

"I can't leave the children."

"Really, Morag! You make me almost glad that stepsister of yours had the gumption to slap you! I have looked after my grandchildren before without any complaints from either of them!"

"But you're playing bridge!"

Dora favoured her with a wry smile. "I told the other ladies I would not be playing at the same time as I rang up the airport. My powers of concentration are more than adequate for normal times, but I doubted that I should play very well this afternoon somehow. I said my daughter-in-law needed me," she added, a glint of amusement in her eyes. "and of course they accepted that my duty to you came first!"

Morag raised a bleak smile. "You're very kind to me," she said.

"Go away!" said Dora, completely exasperated. "Go away and sort yourself out! It's more than time that you did. It isn't only you who likes to give and to be admired for their good nature. Perhaps even Pericles might like to be asked for something for a change!"

"Oh," said Morag.

"Try it!" her mother-in-law recommended. "Try telling him how much you want him to love you, and that it isn't enough for you to love him. Pericles has his doubts too, you know," Dora rammed home her advantage. "He can't do it all by himself!"

Morag licked her lips. "He said I had to tell him in words –" She coloured, suddenly embarrassed. "If you're sure you don't mind having the children, I think I will go out somewhere. I'll take some sandwiches and – and my tent, in case the buses don't fit, so don't worry if I don't come back tonight."

"*I* won't," Dora assured her. "But supposing Pericles

wants to know, which direction do you intend going in?"

Morag opened her mouth, but no words came out. She shook her head and pointed wildly away from the sea. "I don't know – somewhere!"

"Very enlightening!" her mother-in-law mocked."Let's hope Perry can read your mind better than I can!"

CHAPTER TWELVE

MARATHON was hotter than ever. The light breeze that had stirred the dust the last time Morag had been there was absent and there was nothing to ameliorate the burning rays of the sun as they beat down on the narrow street and the huddled white houses on either side. For a while Morag wished she hadn't come. She could have gone anywhere. She could have gone to Eleusis – she might even have found Pericles there before her! But then she still wasn't sure that she was ready to see Pericles quite yet. If he followed her, she supposed she would be glad. No, she amended that to herself, she would be more than glad, she would feel whole again. Her spirits leaped at the thought, only to fall again as she realised that she had no reason to think that he would come looking for her.

She went into the same shop she had been in before and was gratified when its black-clad owner recognised her and produced a bottle of bitter lemon, opening it for her with a flick of her hand. Morag offered her a bank note to pay for it.

"*Téhis psilá?*" the woman asked.

Rightly taking this to mean that she wanted something smaller, Morag searched through her pockets and produced a ten-drachmae coin. The woman nodded happily and took it from her.

Morag drank the bitter lemon slowly, enjoying its chilled qualities as it slid down her dry throat. It was three hours to Rhamnous, if that was where she was going, and there would be no one to give her a lift today.

When she turned to go, picking up her knapsack with one hand, the woman pointed to the necklace of shells round her neck and laughed out loud.

"I don't understand," Morag apologised in Greek. Those few words she had had reason to learn by heart from her phrase book.

"She said you had already been to Rhamnous," a very familiar voice translated behind her.

Morag dropped her knapsack, looking so guilty that her husband laughed at her, touching her scarlet cheeks with an interested hand.

"I thought I'd find you here," he drawled. "Nemesis won't protect you today, however, *agapi mou*. She's on my side in this!"

Morag murmured something quite incomprehensible even to herself, stopped, and made a dash to retrieve her knapsack from the floor. "Did Dora tell you –?"

"My mother was in no state to tell me anything! You've had a busy day, haven't you? Turning the whole family upside down, and blackening my name with them for not treating you better! What she did tell me was that she was looking after the children for some reason instead of playing bridge. Greater love than that, no woman hath!"

Morag stared at him helplessly. "I didn't ask her –" she began. Oh, lord, she thought, was she never going to finish a sentence again? She allowed Pericles to take her knapsack from her and tried to conquer the rising panic within her. "Are you – are you very angry?" she managed to ask.

"That depends," he said dryly. "It depends largely if you are prepared to talk. Are you, Morag?"

She nodded her head quickly, though what she was going to say was beyond her. Her mouth felt dry again, all benefit from the bitter lemon having departed at his words. "Where are we going?"

He looked at her, his eyebrows slightly raised. "To Rhamnous. Where else?"

"If you'd rather go home –"

174

"Would you?"

She shook her head, fingering the green beads in her shell necklace as if they were some kind of charm that could protect her from her own inadequacy.

"I thought not," he said. "Rhamnous will serve us both very well. Perhaps Nemesis will compensate both of us for what we lack in ourselves."

"But you don't lack anything!" she protested. "At least –" The look in his eyes made her feel hot all over – "I don't think you do," she ended, mumbling the words in an agony of embarrassment.

"Don't you, darling?" He lifted her knapsack on to his shoulder and exchanged a few words in rapid Greek with the shopkeeper, accepting a number of bottles of beer and bitter lemon from her. When he had stowed them away in the canvas bag, he put a hand on Morag's shoulder and guided her out of the house. She could feel the strength of his fingers through the thin material of her shirt, and the same elated fear that she felt so often in his presence fountained up within her. "Bravely said," he whispered in her ear, "but it's only a beginning. This time we'll have all the words, if it takes us all night. Agreed?"

Morag wasn't in any position to refuse, even if she had wanted to, and she didn't know that she did. Wasn't that why she had come away by herself? To find the words that he had told her he wanted from her. The truce between them hadn't been enough for her – and perhaps it hadn't been enough for him either. She looked at him uneasily as he opened the door of the car and flung her knapsack on to the rear seat, standing back to allow her to get in.

"I nearly didn't go to Rhamnous," she told him. "I thought of going to Eleusis."

He grinned. "That would have been throwing down the gauntlet with a vengeance. I'll take you there one day, but today I think Rhamnous will suit us better."

A truce was something that could be broken. Had she

broken theirs by sending Delia away? She shivered, marvelling at her own recklessness. But he had come after her, so perhaps he meant to make a final peace with her after all. He would hardly have come if he had only wanted to tell her that he couldn't forgive her gesture of independent defiance of his wishes. She wound her fingers together and her wedding-ring glinted in the sun, startling her into a new line of thought. She was still his wife and, if she played her cards right, she might be able to tempt him into a final peace treaty that neither of them would ever want to break, not ever!

"Yes," she said. She put her head back against the seat and smiled at him. "I brought my tent with me. There's room in it for two – if you don't mind a bit of a squash."

"I think I could bear it." His eyes flickered over her, looking amused. "If you give me the answers I want in time. You won't put me off with a few kisses this time, though. Words are what I want, Morag, if I have to turn you inside out and squeeze them out of you!"

"You – you wouldn't!"

"I would, you know. In fact I'd enjoy doing it, so be very careful, *karthiá mou*. My terms will get steeper the longer you delay."

"The terms for your pride?"

"Amongst other things."

She looked out of the window, watching the famous plain slip past her. She tried to tell herself that she had nothing to be frightened about. Any fool could tell her husband that she loved him! Any fool but her! She didn't know how to begin. But if she didn't tell him, what then?

Pericles put out a hand and patted her knee. "Cheer up, Morag, I'll help you all I can. I don't want to be brutal with you, but neither will I baulk at the last fence. I want us both to know exactly where we stand."

She averted her face, biting her lip. "You're not brutal!"

"No?"

"You know you're not!"

His hand brushed against her hair before returning to the gear-lever. "I was afraid you thought I was the night Kimon lost his coin."

"*Pericles!*" she spluttered.

"What does that mean?"

"You know –" She beat a hasty retreat into silence, hoping that he would let the subject drop.

"Know what?"

"That's why I bought the dress," she brought out jerkily.

"That's why I paid for it!"

Her eyes widened. "Was it? You didn't say anything! I thought – I thought you were being kind because I'd spent everything I had on it!"

"You didn't say anything either," he reminded her, "except that you weren't going to dazzle anyone in particular, and that you'd bought it on impulse."

"But you were being kind too – weren't you?"

"Maybe."

Morag wriggled uncomfortably. "I–I thought you didn't want me – only for the children. The dress was a symbol of – of –"

"Say it, Morag!"

She looked down at her hands in her lap. "That I was willing –"

"Willing, Morag? You'll have to do better than that!"

"I can't!" she said.

She stared sightlessly out of the window, berating herself inwardly for her cowardice. He must know she loved him, so there was no point in not admitting it. She would, she promised herself, but not until she knew if he was angry with her for sending Delia away. Honesty compelled her to admit that this was a mere excuse for procrastination, and she knew that Pericles would recognise it as such.

He was silent too, apparently waiting for her to take the next initiative in the conversation. Perhaps this was her moment for bringing up the subject of Delia. She cast him a speculative look, trying to persuade herself that he might find the story amusing rather than dwell on her own motives for removing her stepsister from his proximity as fast as she possibly could. The strength of his face pleased her, even while she thought it boded ill for her own immediate comfort. He was very good-looking, not in a commonplace way, but like a Greek statue with that curious tactile quality that made one long to touch, even to caress. She looked away quickly, before she could give way to such a temptation.

They had left the Plain of Marathon far behind by now. A large flock of goats came running down a nearby hill and flooded across the road ahead of them. Pericles braked, slowing to a stop. The goat could well be the symbol of Greece, Morag thought. They came from nowhere, going nowhere, following the fluting call of their goatherd, their bells providing the counterpoint to the timeless music of the scene. They had such pretty ears!

"I love Greek goats!" Morag exclaimed.

Pericles eyed her lazily. "Well, you said that easily enough!" he observed.

Instantly she was all confusion. "That's different!" she murmured.

"So I see!"

"Oh, Pericles, don't be beastly!"

"The remedy is in your own hands."

She searched his face looking for some sign that he understood how she felt, but apart from a fleeting flash of amusement in his eyes, he might have been carved from granite.

"I don't understand," she said faintly.

"Oh yes, you do!" He let in the clutch and the car moved slowly forward again. "I won't wait for ever," he added, giving her a look that held so much in it that she felt a great rush of warmth for him.

"I l–love you too!"

"Next best to the goats?"

That struck her as funny and she giggled. "No, I love you best of all!"

He pulled the car into the side of the road, a pleased smile on his lips. "Now that," he said, "deserves some kind of a reward, don't you think? Bravely said, Morag! Was it so very difficult?"

She was a little surprised to find that she had finally said it after all. "I love you very much!" she repeated.

He put a hand on either side of her face, smoothing back her hair with his thumbs. Her green eyes grew almost as dark as his. Then his mouth touched hers in a gentle salute. But, almost immediately, he had put her away from him and had started up the car again, giving all his concentration to the road ahead.

There was no one else at Rhamnous. The ancient shrine slept under the hot sun, disturbed only the occasional bird, hopping over the fallen marble pillars, or soaring in the thermals that surrounded the headland. It was just as beautiful as Morag remembered it. The mountains in the distance rose in rugged grandeur on the other side of the ink-blue sea. The dark, black-green of the pine trees offered a pleasing cool shade from where they could see right over the delightful view that the ruined fort on the headland afforded Pericles, having bought the entry tickets, took Morag by the hand and guided her along the rough path towards the two abandoned temples that had once been the centre of the worship of Nemesis, and Thetis with her interest in justice, custom and equity.

"I brought some sandwiches," Morag said. "They're in my knapsack."

He took them out, placing them carefully on a flat stone and arranging the bottles he had bought around them. "They're a bit squashed. My fault, I'm afraid. I put the beer on top of them. What else have you got in here?"

179

Morag looked away from him. "Not much. Just my night things and – and the tent."

"Ah, yes, the tent!" he grinned. "Weren't you going to get rather hungry if this was all the food you brought with you?"

"I have some money," she explained.

"I'm surprised. Did Delia pay for her own ticket?"

So it had come! The battle had opened with a vengeance and, although she had been expecting it, she felt quite unprepared to deal with it.

"Dora took it out of the housekeeping," she confessed. "I don't think she thought I had enough money to pay for it myself. I wouldn't have had if you hadn't paid for the dress! But you mustn't blame her, Perry! It was all my doing!"

"Was it indeed?"

Morag accepted the sandwich he held out to her, though when she bit into it she couldn't have told if it was ham or fish, or what it was. It was impossible to see what Pericles was thinking, for he had his face turned away from her and all she could see was his thick black hair and the way it curled up at his neck, as if it had a life of its own. What would he do if she were to reach out her hand and give that curl a pull? Would he know the delight she found in touching him and in having him touch her? Her face flamed at the thought.

"Why did you want to take Delia to Eleusis on her own?" she asked him. Her voice sounded husky and very unsure and she gave herself a little mental shake in an attempt to pull herself together. This was no moment for dreaming, she rebuked herself. This was the moment on which her whole future depended.

"To annoy you," he said quietly.

Morag looked at him quickly. "But why?"

He turned his eyes on her, studying her gravely with an enigmatic expression. "I thought it might help you to get it all together. It did, didn't it?"

"I don't know what you mean!" she denied.

"Morag, if you say that once more, I'll take you home now and leave you to stew in your own juice! I'll give you five minutes in which to tell me all about Delia and then we can both forget all about her. She never was as important as you imagined –"

She was to me! Morag kept her tone even with difficulty. She was afraid that she was going to burst into tears. "I saw the way you looked at her when we arrived in England. But it was too late, wasn't it? You were already committed to me, but it was she you wanted to kiss and –" She broke off, horrified by the sight of her own jealousy so plainly revealed for him to see.

"And she would be more than willing to take me from you. Is that it?"

She nodded in earnest now. "But I couldn't let her have *you*! I couldn't, Perry! I'm so sorry, but I couldn't!"

"Didn't it ever occur to you, my love, that I might have had some ideas on the subject? If I'd wanted Delia, don't you think I could have got out of marrying you? I'd had one marriage where neither of us cared very much for the other. Do you think I'd want to go through that again?"

She stopped crying and stared at him. "But you were – you did! I mean, you married me!"

He gave her a mocking look. "Exactly!"

"D–didn't Delia attract you at all?"

The corner of his mouth kicked up into a smile. "Not at all!"

Her eyes widened. "I don't think you should have made use of her like that. She might have got hurt –"

"Unlikely," he decided. "Not that I would have minded inflicting a little pain in that direction. She had done so much to hurt you!"

"But that's nothing to you!" she protested.

"On the contrary," he assured her, "it affects me very

181

dearly. You're my wife, and *no one* hurts you but me! David didn't matter. Anyone with half an eye could see that he had meant nothing to you. He hadn't even kissed you properly –"

"Why told you that?"

He laughed. "You did!"

She remembered that she had, that she had told him that no one had ever kissed her before he had done so, and the memory brought a sweet confusion to her face. Had he known then that she had had no defences against him, but had fallen headlong in love with him at first sight?

She put a hand up to her hot cheeks. "He wasn't particularly interested in that – that side of things," she explained.

"Just as well!" Pericles said. "I prefer to teach my own wife how to make love! But I had to be sure that you weren't being carried away by the emotion of the moment. I wanted you to love me enough to stand up and fight for me, my unselfish darling – and, you see, you did! Even if you had to get my whole family to help you do it, you got rid of Delia!"

"You mean you *wanted* her to go?"

"Well, she isn't my favourite person. I'm sorry to say it about your stepsister, but as a woman she's a pain in the neck!"

Unexpectedly, Morag chuckled and he looked enquiringly at her. "You sounded just like your mother," she said. "I'm sure you both think that a woman is a useless being unless she's subservient to some man!"

The gleam of humour in his eye grew more pronounced. "Don't you?" he mocked her.

"In a way," she admitted. Her eyes met his and her heart jerked within her. The laughter died away from her face and she averted her face hastily in case he should read there of her need for him. The silence stretched her nerves and made it unbearable not to look at him. "Perry –" she began. With a sudden movement she cast herself on

182

her knees beside him. "Perry, I love you. I love you so much it hurts. Please, love me a little bit!" He made as if to speak, but she put up a hand and covered his lips with her fingers. "I know you want me, and – and if that's all, I promise you it'll be enough for me, but –"

His arms went round her in the most satisfactory way. "If that had been all, I wouldn't have made you my wife!" he mocked her. "Travelling round Greece on your own, you were fair game for any wolf who came along."

"I was not! I can look after myself perfectly well –" Her natural honesty made her wonder if that was quite true. She might not have *wanted* to protect herself against Pericles Holmes, no matter what suggestion he had made to her – "Against any one else," she ended meekly, veiling her eyes with her eyelashes and wishing heartily that she had retained a decent silence and not let her indignation get the better of her. "I mean –" she began again on a gulp.

"Your meaning is perfectly clear," he assured her.

"Oh," she said.

His arms tightened about her as she half-heartedly tried to escape his embrace, "Sweetheart, don't you know yet that I feel the same about you? Long before the dress, or my mother's painting of you, I was plotting your downfall. I was afraid I'd put you off me once and for all, but I kept telling myself that you were my wife and that you must have expected me to take you sooner or later. If you were frightened at first, I thought I could overcome that –"

"But – but I was quite willing –" She remembered that he had said she would have to do better than that. "It was wonderful!" she forced out. The words that had always evaded her came tumbling into her mind, and they were somehow easy to say – at least to Pericles. "I couldn't believe it when I first saw you," she said. "You were so beautiful to me! N–not in a feminine sort of way, you could never be that and you know it, but a man can be beautiful, more beautiful than a woman, and I wanted you to make love to me then. You must have known that when you kissed me that time, but after we were married you didn't seem to want me. I thought you were wishing you hadn't, and then I thought perhaps you were Greek enough to think that any woman was better than none, and so I bought the dress and – and made Dora give us the painting, because I thought you'd know then, and it must be rather daunting to have a wife who doesn't – well, you know. But I didn't think it was going to work. It was such a relief when –''

"Then why did you go back to your own room?" he asked her.

"I wanted to be more to you after all. I wanted you to love me too!"

He held her away from him, looking deep into her eyes. "I think you were afraid too," he said. "You looked scared stiff when I threatened to drive you up into the mountains and make love to you there."

Her eyelashes veiled her green eyes for an instant, but then she looked back at him. "I was afraid I wouldn't know how to please you," she confessed, "and I was shy. I'm still a little afraid of you. You see, I never knew that one could feel like this about anyone and – and it takes a bit of getting used to!"

His hand grasped the nape of her neck in a possessive gesture. "Darling Morag," he whispered, "I love you, love you, love you, like I've never loved any other woman, nor ever shall. But I had to be sure that you loved me too. I knew my mother would tell you all about Susan, and I didn't want to be another lame dog for you to break your heart over because you're made that way! I was scared of being another David to you, someone you would give up in an excess of generosity, if Delia and I looked like being attracted to one another. I'll never get over the moment when I got home today and found you'd stood up to her and meant to cling on to me no matter what!"

She smiled, her eyes very bright. "Did that pay for your

pride, Perry?"

He kissed her lips. "I hope you think it's worth it. My pride was lacerated by Susan's indifference. You are quite right, my love, it is daunting to mean less than nothing to the woman in your arms. But with you not even a passionate physical response was enough for me. I wanted your heart and mind as well!"

"They're yours," she answered. "I only want to belong to you, Perry nothing more. Where you lead, I want to follow – with love. Because I don't think I can live without you. Without you, everything is dust and ashes, and only you can make it all glorious for me like – like being born again!"

He held her close, a look that she had never seen before on his face. "Morag, *agapi mou*, for someone who is afraid of words, you can make them sing a lyrical song when you try." He kissed her slowly, his mouth lingering against her soft, parted lips. "Will you forgive me for making you say them?"

Her arms slipped up round his neck and her fingers buried themselves in his hair, luxuriating in the feel of it. "Oh, Perry, don't you know yet how it is with me? You said you wanted the words – all of them, and I nearly died at the thought, but your will is mine, and I knew I'd have to find them in the end if I wanted – your signature on the final peace treaty. And I do! You don't know how much I do!"

"On my terms?" he whispered.

She nodded helplessly, scarcely aware of the gentle way he held her. "On your terms," she agreed. "Because I love you!" She tipped up her face for his kiss. "On any terms," she said, and she was no longer ashamed of the hunger in her voice.

The sun was setting and the boy who looked after the site had appeared from nowhere, a knowing grin on his face.

"We close now," he said. "But you can come back in the

morning. We very seldom have any visitors in the early morning."

Pericles grinned. "It sounds as though we've got our marching orders," he said. "Did you mean it when you offered me the sanctuary of your tent?"

"Yes, of course." Morag gave him a shy look. "But if you'd rather go home –?"

"Certainly not! I intend to have you to myself for a few hours at least before we have Mama preening herself that she did the whole thing on her own, and the children claiming all your attention, thinking that you belong to them–"

"But I do!" she laughed. "I want them to think that. It wouldn't do to exclude them! Besides, I like them." She clamped her mouth shut, determined to say no more, but then she smiled and gave him the victory. "Kimon has a smile just like yours," she confided.

"My dear girl," he said, his eyes very bright, "if that's all it takes to make you happy. I'll have to see what I can do! Though I rather hope that we manage to reproduce that guilty look of yours as well."

"I'd like that," she murmured, determined not to let him see that he had embarrassed her. "But only if Kimon and Peggy don't mind!" She put her hand in his. "Every child should come first with both parents. It's horrible when you don't!"

His fingers stroked her cheek. "I don't think the twins have anything to worry about. You'll find room for them all in that loving heart of yours. I'll vouch for that. Shall we go and get a meal in Marathon, and then come back and make our camp on the headland, outside the old town there?"

She nodded, becoming aware of the boy who was still waiting for them to go. "There's something I must do first, though. I have something for Nemesis, as a kind of thank-you, because she did give us a handsome measure of joy

186

today. I wouldn't like her to think we weren't grateful."

"Are you afraid she'll take it all away again?" he teased her.

"No," she said, but she didn't sound particularly certain. "But I wouldn't want her to think me guilty of *hubris* either!"

He laughed and said something to the boy in Greek. The two of them stood side by side and watched her as she mounted the high step on to the floor of the ruined temple that had been dedicated to Nemesis so many hundreds of years before. There was a place a little towards one end where, probably, once her votive statue had stood, the only one extant where we know what the original looked like and haven't had to guess from later copies.

Morag stood quite still for a long moment, savouring the moment. It was likely, she thought, that she would never be quite as happy as she was at that moment. No one could live on the peaks all their life, nor would she want to, but neither would she have been without this one day when Pericles had said he loved her.

She took the shells from around her neck and laid them carefully on the ground in front of her.

She stood up, and smiled at Pericles, and remembered a speech she had once learned from the *Eumenides*. She thought it was Athena's command to the Furies when they had agreed to settle in her land.

"*Blessings*," she quoted, "*in harmony with a victory that has no evil in it: blessings from the earth and from the waters of the sea and from the sky. And you must pray that the wind's breath may pass across my land in sunlight; that the fruits of the earth and increase of grazing beasts, abundant, thriving, may not fail my citizens in time to come; and that the seed of man may be kept safe.*"

Pericles came to the edge of the temple and lifted her down, with a smile as intimate as her own.

"Amen to that," he said.

187

Mills & Boon Classics

The very best of Mills & Boon
romances, brought back for those of you
who missed reading them when they
were first published.

There are three other Classics for you to collect this
December

HEART OF THE LION
by Roberta Leigh

When Philippa encouraged young Cathy Joyce to elope,
she didn't know the girl was the niece of her boss, the
formidable newspaper tycoon Marius Lyon — but that
didn't stop him promptly giving her the sack. But that
was by no means the last of Marius as far as Philippa
was concerned!

THE IRON MAN
by Kay Thorpe

When Kim had no news of her fiancé in the Sierra Leone
she decided to go and find out what had happened to
him. And encountered opposition in the shape of the
domineering Dave Nelson who told her, 'Don't run away
with the notion that being female gives you any special
immunity where I'm concerned'.

THE RAINBOW BIRD
by Margaret Way

Paige Norton was visiting the vast Benedict cattle empire
as the guest of Joel Benedict. She had looked forward to
it immensely, although she hadn't much liked the sound
of Joel's stepbrother Ty, the boss of the station. And
when she met Ty, she liked the reality even less ...

If you have difficulty in obtaining any of these books through
your local paperback retailer, write to:

Mills & Boon Reader Service
P.O. Box 236, Thornton Road, Croydon, Surrey, CR9 3RU.

Mills & Boon Classics

The very best of Mills & Boon
romances, brought back for those of you
who missed reading them when they
were first published

In
January
we bring back the following four
great romantic titles.

FAMILIAR STRANGER
by Lilian Peake

Adrienne was determined to marry her fiancé, Clifford Denning
— but was 'determination' the right attitude to take to something
as important as marriage? Clifford's brother Murray kept warning
her that she was heading for disaster but why should she listen to
that overbearing Murray?

BRIDE'S DILEMMA
by Violet Winspear

Tina married John Trecarrel in haste — and had time to repent
when she found out that she had to compete with the memory
of his beautiful first wife and that he was attracted to Joanna's
equally beautiful cousin Paula.

THE YELLOW MOON
by Rebecca Stratton

It was going to break Catherine's heart to be forced to send her
two adored little half-brothers to live with their unknown Greek
uncle on his Greek island home. Then it appeared that this uncle
was planning to take over Catherine's life as well . . .

WITCHSTONE
by Anne Mather

When Ashley's father died she travelled northwards to live with
her uncle and aunt in their hotel. There she met Jake, to whom she
was attracted, but who had to be remote for many reasons . . .
most of all because of his forthcoming marriage to Barbara.

If you have difficulty in obtaining any of these books through
your local paperback retailer, write to:

Mills & Boon Reader Service
P.O. Box 236, Thornton Road, Croydon, Surrey, CR9 3RU.

The Mills & Boon Rose is the Rose of Romance

Every month there are ten new titles to choose from — ten new
stories about people falling in love, people you want to read
about, people in exciting, far-away places. Choose Mills & Boon.
It's your way of relaxing:

December's titles are:

KING OF COPPER CANYON *by Elizabeth Graham*
Dani had gone to confront Grant King, but instead she found
herself holed up with a disreputable character named Burt . . .

SEASON OF SHADOWS *by Yvonne Whittal*
Laura had become mother to her dead sister's child, but the girl
also needed a father. Could Laura go through with a marriage to
Anton DeVere?

THE LAST NIGHT AT PARADISE *by Anne Weale*
Arriving in the Caribbean to find her grandfather had died, Amalie
was forced to accept the help of the mysterious Blake . . .

COMPULSION *by Charlotte Lamb*
Why was Lissa so reluctant to marry Chris? Shouldn't she be far
more wary of the mysterious, reckless Luc Ferrier?

ENGAGED TO JARROD STONE *by Carole Mortimer*
Temper had provoked Brooke into declaring her 'engagement' to
Jarrod Stone — and it suited him to make the engagement a real
one!

DARK SURRENDER *by Margaret Pargeter*
The more Julie knew of Brad Hewson the more she realised that
any woman who was foolish enough to love him was doomed
to be hurt . . .

A DREAM OF THEE *by Mary Wibberley*
After the way Lachlan Erskine had treated her, Catriona had
kept her distance from men — but now Lachlan had turned up
again . . .

REUNION AT PITEREEKA *by Kerry Allyne*
Why was Rebel's brother on such bad terms with Chayne
Cavanagh, the man she had come to love? She just had to find out.

THE SPANISH UNCLE *by Jane Corrie*
How could Mary give up looking after her dead sister's small son
when the boy's uncle, Rafael Alvarados, made it clear that he
wanted him?

SOUTHERN NIGHTS *by Janet Dailey*
When Todd Gaynor took his fiancée Barbara home to meet his
family, she found herself confronted with the last man in the
world she wanted to see . . .

If you have difficulty in obtaining any of these books from your
local paperback retailer, write to:

Mills & Boon Reader Service
P.O. Box 236, Thornton Road, Croydon, Surrey, CR9 3RU.

Give yourself and your friends a romantic Christmas.

First time in paperback, four superb romances
by favourite authors, in an attractive maroon and
old gift pack. A superb present to give. And to receive.

Mills & Boon

**First Time
in Paperback
Four Favourite
Authors**

Sandstorm	**Lord of the High Valley**
Anne Mather	Margaret Way
Man's World	**Enemy In Camp**
Charlotte Lamb	Janet Dailey

United Kingdom £2.60
Rep. of Ireland £2.86
Publication 10th October 1980

Look for this gift pack at your local Mills & Boon stockist.

 The Mills & Boon rose is the rose of romance